ALSO BY ALEX CLERMONT

Eating Kimchi and Nodding Politely
Missing Rib

YOU, ME
AND THE
REST OF US

#NewYorkStories

ALEX
CLERMONT

You, Me and the Rest of Us:
#NewYorkStories

Some of these stories first appeared in *The Bodega Monthly* annual anthology, *Scholars & Rogues*, *Every Second Sunday*, *Foliate Oak*, *The Other Herald*, *the ao12* annual anthology, and AlexClermontWrites.com

Dedicated/Thank You

THESE STORIES ARE dedicated to my brother Joesly, and the many other New Yorkers who's lives I snatched pieces of to put together this collection of stories about the city I love and hate.

New York is the city I grew up in and the city that, no matter where I live, will always be my home. Thank you to every person, and to every piece of metal, brick and glass that makes New York City more than the sum of its parts.

-Alex Clermont

TABLE OF CONTENTS

REAL WORDS
(A PROLOGUE)

ABE READ HIS POEM for the twenty-third time. With each pass his opinion of it hopped from one side of the fence to the other, unsure if what he had written was totally worthless or if bits and pieces could be salvaged and turned into something beautiful. After his twenty-second read, however, he was firmly on the side of totally worthless.

Abe was required to take Poetry Workshop 101 in order to get his BA in journalism. He failed it the first time and found himself doomed to repeat it if he wanted to graduate. This time he made a real effort, and for two weeks he read pieces by the likes of Pinkney and Bernard Shaw; he fought off boredom in class, and the sleepiness it brought on; when writing, Abe tried his best to stay away from haikus about the true nature of the suffering, which was the first thing he thought of when he thought of poetry.

It all culminated on the uptown 6 train where he had

finished putting together his first poem. After a few nights of enjambments and delicate word insertions, Abe came up with a page of lines that, by accident, formed the shape of a penis or a rocket. In the end, however, he decided that it was just crap.

As he saw it, the ethereal phrases that filled his tablet's screen were so vague that they could mean anything, though ultimately they said nothing. They were his best imitation of what he *thought* Shakespeare would write if he were a Jew, born in the late 1990s, and living in Spanish Harlem with his activist girlfriend and their adjunct professor roommate.

> *The vastness of*
> *the space between us*
> *fills me with a longing for*
> *the tenderness of contact that*
> *has always escaped my reach.*

In some of his re-readings, he liked the way this particular sentence sounded. But what did it mean, exactly? Did it express anything about the world around him? His answer was no. It just sounded nice, and nowhere near nice enough.

If he showed the effort, would the professor give him a passing grade? Maybe, but he couldn't let graduation teeter on good enough. The problem was that he didn't know what to do with the half-full screen in front of him.

Abe lifted his head to look around the crowded train and at the spectacle that his city put on display. His view was filled with hard and metal things he wasn't inspired to write haikus about. He noticed the smell of a sleeping drunk whose appearance created an almost physical bubble that no one dared enter—even in the packed, rush-hour full, subway car. On the opposite end, he saw the wonder and energy of a squirming infant being breastfed by its mother. He noticed lovers, loud teens, and tired workers. Metaphors using abstractions and celestial bodies didn't move Abe as much as opening his eyes to the people he shared the world with.

He trashed the week-old document with a tap on his screen and began anew. He tried his best to put together words that described how it felt to walk out of his front door that morning and see not only the different shades of people walking the streets, but also the beautiful New York City skyline built by poor immigrants. He thought about the place his grandparents had escaped from, only to continue their same habits in a different country and city.

The life Abe knew was full of circles and contradictions that he wanted the world to know about. His 116th Street stop was coming up soon, but Abe didn't move. He stayed in his seat and continued to write about what was real.

POINT OF VIEW

MY GRANDMOTHER GAVE BIRTH to a dozen children in her hometown of Dorchester, South Carolina—a place full of space, but lacking in contraceptives. When I was thirteen, my mother pulled me aside after school to show me pictures she had found of her mother. I looked at the photos of the woman who had raised her but felt no connection to the curly hair, the beady eyes, or loose jowls.

Before then I had already cemented in my mind a picture of my grandmother as a haggard, Dust Bowl-era old lady in a sundress who was perpetually pregnant. I pictured a toothless smile as each one of my aunts and uncles popped out of her body holding a bright little ball of life energy that they had stolen during birth, leaving her, and Dorchester, behind. My grandmother's kids took to the wind and planted their roots across the country like dandelion seeds.

The oldest ones sent her money and visited every so often

while the youngest one, my mother, grew up in Dorchester until it was her turn to leave. That time never came and I grew up in the same place she did. I grew up in the same place my grandmother did—an unrecognizable woman who at looked me from faded photos she took in my backyard, decades ago.

My mother asked me to stand next to her as she browsed through the album on our kitchen table, but she eventually gave me a kiss before letting me leave. What I thought when I saw those images of stoic stares and hard scrabble living was the same thing I thought today as I hit the road: I've got to escape this place.

It was something like being at a party when you realize that you don't really like anybody there. I lived in a place that was uncomfortably tolerable. I was uncomfortable with waking up and having each day be like the one before. I was uncomfortable with the fact that social activities all revolved around eating or sports. As much as my mother loved me, I was uncomfortable being the boy who liked boys in a town where last century's social stigmas hadn't entirely disappeared. I wanted beautiful experiences and unique settings, but I had fields of tall grass. I needed to escape. For five years I did just that at SC State where I got a bachelor's degree for "playing with computers," as my mother would call it.

While there I fell for a skinny man with mousy hair who held me after making love in a way that let me know I was cared for. I made friends, and was invited to at least one tech geek dinner party where someone brought up the name Niklaus Wirth. I argued with one of the nerds about using the spacebar versus the tab key when writing code, and almost punched him in the mouth after four beers.

I was grateful for almost every minute of it, but after graduation I was back in Dorchester and looking for a career while holding a job as a manager at a local diner called *Pete's*.

I was getting a small belly from constantly snacking on fried chicken and not moving my body beyond the limited requirements of my job. As with the photo album, my mother waited until I got home from work one day to ask me, "You remember your Uncle Jonathan?"

"How old was I when he was here last?"

"I'd say you were probably five."

"Ah. Then, no, I don't remember him."

"Well, he gave me a call last night to see what I've been up to."

With a face coated in burger grease, I said, "Okay," and hoped that the exchange would finish quickly so that I could run to the shower and scrub the day's work off me.

"He's living in New York City now, and it seems like he's been doing lots of things involving technology. He likes playing with computers, just like you."

"Really?"

"Yes. So we got to talking about your situation and he says, 'maybe I can help Paul out. You should have him give me a call.' Don't know exactly what he can do, except maybe point you in the right direction or just give you some good advice. Whatever it is, we didn't pay all that money just so you could help the fry cook when it gets busy."

"You're right, Ma. I'll give him a call in the morning. Thanks for always thinking about me." Though I didn't put any faith in the idea, I kissed her on the corner of her warm smile and felt glad that, though I had no one else, I had her.

The next morning I did as I said I would and called my uncle Jonathan. He spoke in condensed bursts of words carried with an accent that made me picture a crooked politician on the other end of the phone—twirling a cigar between his fingers and grinning arrogantly. Despite the seedy figure of him that popped up, John, as he asked me to call him, was very helpful and bluntly honest.

"Yeah, no that degree not worth shit, Michael. You and Iris paid for some money for fancy paper."

"If you say so, Uncle John."

"It's not about what I say, but what I can observe. The guy who invented the autocorrect on your phone has a bachelor's in history. Not many successful programmers have formal training. They're self taught."

"I'm sure that's true, but for right now I do have a degree in computer sciences that I'd like to put to use." It felt strange using so many words in a sentence compared to John's short chunks.

He said, "Nothing wrong with that. Let ask you, though, what languages do you know?"

"Um, Python, Java, Ruby, C, C++, CSS…"

"Sounds like you've got your shit together. Are you expert in all of them?"

"Yeah, though I'm a little rusty on C."

"No biggie. Most of us are. Okay, so I'm gonna give you some names and numbers. Get ready to take them down."

I grabbed my cracked tablet and typed about fifteen different names of people and companies along with their phone numbers. John told me that he personally knew all of them and if they liked what I had to say they'd find something for me. "Don't make me look bad." he chuckled, right after I thanked him.

After a week I ended up with an over-the-phone interview for a position with an online media company. I nervously gripped my phone with clammy fingers as I answered their questions--not noticing how hot I was until sweat flew off my face when I turned to face my computer screen.

They asked for a face-to-face interview. I managed to get three others as well. John offered me his place and said that if things worked out he would get me in touch with an agent to find a decent apartment out there.

When I hung up the phone that last time, my hand trembled and it took a full fifty seconds for it to stop. Life was changing. I was going to move to New York.

Mom had her church to keep her company, so I didn't feel too guilty as I spent my Friday morning heaving boxes of clothing and electronics into my car. At seventy-five miles per hour I drove past cornfields on my way to New York City.

My phone's "90s Grungy Grunge" playlist was booming out of the archaic car stereo system on the way up north. The volume was at chassis shaking levels to help keep me awake during the long trip, but the frayed power and volume wires added would every-so-often disconnect and add a second of dead silence which had the effect of a tranquilizer.

Having driven for ten hours and being awake for about twenty-one, I was reaching my limits. It wasn't to the point where I had to get off the road and sleep in my car like a hobo on wheels, but I would be at that point soon. I chanced it and kept driving. After shaking my head to bring me back to my high-speed reality, I narrowed my eyes and kept them on the road in front of me.

The nighttime darkness didn't make the trip any easier. It put up a black curtain that blocked out everything beyond the borders of the highway road so that even with my high beams on all I could see was asphalt up ahead—its white lane dividers flashed hypnotically the faster I drove. Taking a quick glance down at my phone's GPS notification, I could see that I was only two hours away. I figured I could hold out for that long.

It was one a.m. and there was no real traffic on the highway. The occasional car drove past but generally, I was alone. I wondered if I should make a stop at the next rest area and get a Red Bull, a Blue Dragon, a Green Puke—something to lift my energy level up a bit. I decided that I couldn't waste the time and changed the playlist for the sake of variety. After a few rap songs about guns and jewelry, I heard "our" song and it made me think about why I was getting to New York so late in the first place.

Ken lived in a Charlotte suburb. Living well too, from what I gathered. Right out of college he had gotten a job as a producer's assistant at one of the local networks. I knew this because after we broke up we were still on speaking terms and promised to stay that way. We kept that promise too—at least online. We followed each other on social media where we would occasionally comment or "like" at a rate of about once every three weeks. I did the math.

I tried not to feel heartbroken when I checked my newsfeed on a rainy Saturday to see pictures of him with another man. When those pictures disappeared a few months later, I tried not to dance on my bed. There was a lot of trying, but we hadn't seen each other since he told me after graduation that he loved me, but couldn't see us going on like we were.

He said this on our last visit to his parent's place, and on their front porch I asked what the hell he meant. I might have yelled it if his father wasn't within shouting distance. He told me that he didn't feel comfortable being himself with me. He wasn't happy holding back. He said I drained him sometimes.

It sounded like bullshit, and I took the whole thing as hard as you'd expect a love struck, brand new adult to take being dumped. I thought about it since, though, and in retrospect his fluffy world of art and yoga was always alien to me. I was looking from the outside in, to a place where Jean Michel Basquiat was a great artist; a community where Jackson Pollock's seemingly random and talentless paint splotches were more than just paint splotches. I was content with that dynamic, but I supposed he needed more.

He read my post about driving to New York City and, staying in line with the online parameters of our new friendship, he sent me an instant message that rang in my headphones as I was writing computer code to impress potential bosses. The message asked if I wanted to pay him a visit on my way up. He was hoping to say goodbye in person before I left the South altogether. I replied. He gave me his address.

I reached Ken's place at noon and met him at the door with a smile that he reciprocated without hesitation. We drove to a restaurant in the city for lunch, immersed in the comfortable atmosphere of people who knew far too much about each other to feel awkward.

Over some very good eggs Benedict, Ken said, "I was shocked. To just up and drop everything you've got going to chase a maybe across the country. And to *New York City*, no less. What got into you?" My relaxed attitude was always a strange contrast to Ken's upbeat nature. Maybe it was another thing he couldn't see lasting forever. I calmly took a sip of my iced tea and said, "It's not that crazy. Things look pretty promising, and if it doesn't work out I'm sure Ned's will rehire me."

"How do you manage to make something so exciting seem so boring?" He shook his head with a smile, like I had just shrugged my shoulders at the Mona Lisa. He picked up his toast and sopped up some of the runny egg at edge of his plate. He chewed as I sipped.

"Are you happy at least?"

"Very. I've got a decent chance of living out my dream. I mean, just adding to my portfolio made me grin. Knowing that it's gonna be seen and lead directly to the life I've always wanted."

"And what's that?" he asked, already knowing.

"To work as a programmer." His smile widened, forcing me to continue. "To *leave* Dorchester."

"Well, if you're not excited about that, then I'll be excited for you. Dreams are capricious, though. Things may work out differently in the real world with real people who are looking at things from their own perspective."

"Doesn't sound like we're talking about me anymore."

"Oh, we are. I'm just saying that if you're gonna try looking at the world as an optimist for the first time, wear some shades. There's a lot you can't see when the sun's in your eyes."

We continued talking about New York and he asked me to take a picture of the Stonewall Inn for him. I promised I would. Except for our past together, we talked about everything. Near the end he explained to me the disillusionment with his current job, and the fact that he wasn't just giving me helpful advice about dreams while chewing his egg-soaked toast. I listened and tried to be a better friend than I was a boyfriend.

When I drove Ken home later that afternoon we sat in my car and laughed about Susie Rebado. She was the chemistry class idiot who ended up fucking her way to a cushy career as the senator's daughter-in-law. A stay-at-home wife, her only job was to occasionally blow the senator's son—maybe make a baby.

Ken and I both saw that, or something like that, in her future. We didn't blame her for it though. Born gorgeous and dirt poor, there was very little she was expected to do other than make some straight man feel good. It was at her freshman dorm party that I met Ken. She gave him a drunken kiss that he quickly ended by backing away a foot or three into me. He apologized with a smirk and introduced himself. Only a minute into conversation Susie played "Back That Azz Up." Everyone went wild and Ken turned around to shake his ass at me. It became our song.

In my car we laughed about it, and he said that he used to get such a kick out of how prudish I was. When he started grinding against my waist he could feel my erection, but could also see the uncomfortable expression on my face.

He said he loved that look.

With those words our laughter subsided in acknowledgement of the fact that we were crossing a line. I still loved him, but he made it clear, even before we officially broke up, that I didn't make him happy. I never could.

We had talked enough, and with both of us smiling cordially to each other, we said goodbye. I assumed it was for the last time and got back on the highway to New York City.

My phone was dying. The faulty power cable had decided to give its last bit of charge thirty minutes ago. The only call I had made was to my uncle to let him know I'd be coming in late. The real energy drain was coming from the GPS, which was lowering the battery's power at a rate of about one percent every two minutes. I turned the GPS off intermittently, but when I got onto the New Jersey Turnpike I had to keep it on so I knew what exits to get off. By the time I reached New York City my phone was at seven percent.

I forgot the number as soon the reality of where I was hit me. The "Welcome To New York" sign was all I could think about. I was there. I was here. I had arrived. I was a tourist, but hopefully I'd soon be a resident. To appreciate it a little more, I slowed down and looked at the landscape through cautious glances. Lots of homes that took suburban living in a direction I hadn't see before. Pretty houses in small spaces built with an architectural eye unfamiliar to my time in Dorchester, or even Charlotte for that matter.

The signs told me I was heading to the Verrazano Bridge. I drove over it through Brooklyn and into Manhattan where my uncle stayed. Everything looked so radically different from what I was used to. TV shows let me know what to expect, but seeing a crowd of background extras in a cop drama was nothing like driving by a subway train station and gawking at the eclectic mix of outsiders and conformists; seeing a postcard of the New York skyline was nothing like driving over the Brooklyn Bridge and seeing the expanse of skyscrapers lit up like stars by their own light. I was in love.

The area where my uncle lived was called the West Village, and I was to call him when I got close. The problem was that my phone was dead. I began to panic a little but didn't let it dampen my mood. I had the address on good old-fashioned paper and had no problem figuring out the grid design of the city. I drove slow and marveled some more.

John's neighborhood had a pretty mix of dirty and pristine. Late night coffee shops and hip sushi bars crowded around each other, next to a public square that, upon closer inspection at a red traffic light, housed a mini tent city and wooden benches spotted with bird droppings. That scene was only a few avenues away from where John lived—a quiet side street lined with trees and antique townhouses. Based on my little bit of research I expected the parking situation to be just as horrible as it was. It took me twenty minutes to find a spot and try my hand at parallel parking for the second time in my life. At 1:30 a.m. the avenues were still bustling with people and, for the first time since leaving Charlotte, I smiled.

The life around me was nothing like my world in Dorchester, where your home could be a two-minute drive away from your neighbor's. I thought about those desolate places and how I never noticed them as such when I was growing up. I tried to explain my realization to the chef at Ned's over a few beers after work.

Sitting on the hood of my car I asked Jimmy, "Do you like people?"

He laughed, "Kinda question is that?" After taking a swig from his beer he said, "Some people I like, some I don't. You asking about the new waitress? She's kinda cute."

"Hadn't noticed. No, I just mean that some people really like being alone. The things that other people do annoy them. You know? We talk loud. We're messy. We all like different things. We misunderstand each other all the time. Some people just don't wanna deal with that. They don't like other people."

"I think I know what you're saying. I know a few folks who'd like nothing better than to be alone in their little house. Come out only for food and water. Reckon I got a cousin like that. See him only at funerals."

"Exactly. Some people just don't like other people. Sometime I wish I was like that, but I need to be around people. I love just talking, or even arguing, or anything that lets me know that it's not just me out here. Like, even with your cousin, he's probably a mean sonofabitch, but we're all the same really. We're just all doing what we think is best. We're all trying to get by. Even the worst of us have something special that just went wrong. That's the way I look at it and when you see things like that it's hard not to want to be around folks who are all just trying to figure out things along with you." Jimmy nodded and took another gulp. I said, "When I was in college there were all kinds of things happening. People were laughing, partying, studying, talking, just spending time together. Even when people were angry, there was a closeness. A feeling that I could reach out and there would be another person there. Back here, though, I feel so disconnected. There's so little happening that we can all get together on. We're just so far apart."

"I told you about football down at Fort Dorchester High. Everybody's there."

I sighed and said, "Not exactly what I was going for. They do have a good team, though."

"Hell yeah they do."

I finished the beer I had been swinging between my bent knees and looked up. The sky was clear of clouds and filled with stars. The thick arm of the Milky Way stretched across our view as we gazed and drank a few more beers. It was beautiful, but it reminded me that there was so much space around us. It was liberating and constrictive at the same time. Parked on the side of that road, I could've thrown that beer bottle in any direction and no one besides me or Jimmy would have heard it.

I looked at the address on my notepad to make sure it matched the number on the door I was looking at. It did and I pressed the buzzer. I waited a minute and buzzed again. Thirty seconds after that, I pressed the buzzer a third time, thinking that, surely, he just hadn't heard me the first two times. Ten buzzes and seven minutes later I realized that I was not getting in.

A feeling of fear spread from my spine to the rest of my body, forcing me to asked some scary questions: What if I had the wrong address? What if John had forgotten about me and took a vacation to another country? What if John was dead somewhere—hit head-on by a crazy New York City cab driver? With my phone dead I was in the dark. I panicked about what I was going to do in a city this big where I knew nobody.

My choices were to either sit on the townhouse stoop and wait, or explore the city and then come back to check the door again. The second, full of promising distractions, seemed like a better idea. With a deep breath I stepped onto Sixth Avenue, still deathly tired from my long drive.

I planned to take a circular mini tour, ending back at my uncle's front door an hour after leaving it. My first step on the path put me onto a busy avenue that exposed a straight line up almost the entire island of Manhattan. It was lit up by the bright lights of advertisements and store signs asking me to buy products or join a club.

I yawned and walked past several late night stores. One of them had a dildo hanging behind the window like meat at a butcher's. I stopped when I noticed it and giggled to myself like a kid seeing a pornography magazine for the first time. It was a sex shop, and it was my first time seeing one. Before walking inside I stared at the dildo a little more. It was purple, average sized and dotted with rounded bumps that were spread uniformly throughout. I wondered how someone would think that could feel good and so, with Ken's comment about me stepping doing something different, I decided to go inside and ask the clerk.

She looked at me intensely as I walked through the door, and with a smile said, "We close in another ten minutes, ginger."

"Oh, okay," I said with an unease that seemed to suddenly appear after being confronted by a stranger. "I was just curious. I've never been inside a place like this before."

Her smile grew into a grin and she said, "I love your accent! Where are you from?"

"South Carolina. Although…" I coughed, "I'm probably gonna be moving here soon."

She walked up to me and, looking at my hair instead of my eyes, said, "Well, ginger, I don't know much about South Carolina, but I think you're making the right choice in moving here. Now, what were you curious about?"

I smiled awkwardly, "Just saw the, uh, uh, the device at the window and I wanted to look around a little."

"You're looking for a dildo?"

"No! I mean, I was just looking *at* one."

"Okay. Well, we're got a few of them. What are you into?"

"I, um. I like…" I began to sweat a little. Nothing terrible, but it was noticeable.

She walked back to the register and said, "Why don't you just take a look around?"

I nodded and browsed around the small shop with its pink painted ceiling and oddly shaped objects of all sorts. I was startled by the buzzing of a vibrator that I had turned on by mistake. Fake penises modeled after adult film stars lined one of the walls, and I found myself totally unaroused—as well as a little freaked out. I turned around and slowly walked to the door of the small store. The clerk said, "Here" as she gave me a store business card. "Come in tomorrow. I'm sure we'll find something you like." I nodded as I took the card and said, "Thanks." Putting it in my pants pocket, I walked out and back onto the sidewalk.

Kids, probably no more than fourteen years old, were sitting on the curb outside, even though it was past 2 a.m. They were drinking and smoking and skateboarding. A multiracial bunch, worthy of an urban teen drama, they sported unique clothes and strange haircuts that they showed off nonchalantly. I strolled by and stared at the scene, which would have been unthinkable to me a few hours before.

The unthinkable confronted me on every other corner in metropolitan scenes that rubbed raw my modest upbringing. I stopped, stared, and gawked at buildings and people. Everything was different, and some things were disturbingly so a little disturbing.

Most of the storefronts were closed, but I passed by a twenty-four hour restaurant called Papaya King that smelled and looked like a hot dog stand. With no papayas in site—and no desire for a papaya—I walked in and looked at the menu. A look of impatience was all I got from the cook who eventually asked, "What you want?"

"A hot dog, I guess. With, uh, with everything."

"Okay buddy." He immediately turned around and began to work the grill. About ten seconds later a ragged man walked in—both his hair and clothes were in discolored knots that looked to have been smeared in mud. He walked with an off-balanced shuffle and just the sight of him l let me know I was looking at the most wretched human being on earth. His putrid body odor filled the modest dining area in seconds, and he quickly walked to the condiments area. He was hollering incoherent sentence fragments while waving his hands—catching the eye of the cook.

I noticed all of this in the short time it took him to walk to the soda fountain next to the ketchup and mustard. He grabbed the ketchup bottle and squeezed it into his mouth. The chef began walking from behind the counter as the homeless man put his hand under the ice dispenser. He dropped his pants and began shoving ice cubes into his asshole while yelling insanities about Jesus and titties.

The cook yelled, "What the fuck are you doing?" and pushed the man with his gloved hands. More nonsense was yelled, but the man didn't fight back as the cook pushed him out of the restaurant and onto the sidewalk. "If you in here again, I'ma kick your fucking ass!" Coming back in he said to me, "Sorry 'bout that."

Without another word I walked out stunned as if I'd just been dunked in ice water, or had ice cubes shoved in my asshole. I kept walking, silent and scared, until I hit some small corporate green area between two buildings. I ran as deep as I could into it and sat on the bench. I could still see people walking by, but tree branches masked their shape. The figures were more silhouettes than solid humans.

I leaned back and breathed in deeply as my fatigue from

twenty-four hours of consciousness began to overwhelm me. What the hell had I gotten myself into? Who the hell are these people? What kind of place was I now stuck in? Where could I go if I couldn't take it here, but couldn't stand it in Dorchester either? I tried to calm myself by looking up—away from the shapes beyond the trees. The sky was so different from the one I knew. The stars were missing and in their place were the artificial lights from towering skyscrapers.

I kept breathing and just leaned back on the bench. These were going to be my people. This was going to be my town. I had to realize that the folks I grew up with, the holy people, the sinners, the prosperous and the desperate, were all people just like *these* people. No matter the actions, they were trying to do the best with what they had, just like me.

I relaxed on the bench as I reminded myself of what I already knew. With a quiet yawn, I got up to walk to my uncle's place and sleep on his stoop. I stood for a few seconds outside the park to gather up the strength to fight the sleepiness that was overtaking me. A stranger stopped as he passed me, and with a quizzical look asked if I was all right. I said, "Not really, but I thank you for asking."

With concern on his face, as if he saw blood coming down my nose, he said, "I can call an ambulance if you need me to."

"No, thank you," I said wondering how horrible I looked to get that kind of response from a stranger. I thought again and then said, "Actually, would you mind if I used your phone to call someone? I'm from out of town, and a little lost out here with my phone dead."

His concern turned into suspicion as he handed me his phone and said, "Okay."

I tried my best to remember my uncle's phone number. Through the fog of sleep deprivation, I grabbed a few digits and dialed. Three rings later I heard his voice, "Hello. Who is this?"

"Hey, John. It's Paul. Your nephew."

"Whoa! What happened to you? I've been calling for like the last two hours. You didn't get my text messages?"

"No, my phone's dead. I'm calling from a stranger's phone right now." I smiled at the man whose phone I was using. "Are you home?"

"I am now. There was an emergency with a client and I had to leave." After a short pause, he said, "You let your phone die?" It was said in a way that implied I'd done something as stupid as forget to breathe.

"I'll see you in a few, Uncle John."

"Okay."

Handing the phone back to the man I said, "Thank you, sir. I really needed that."

"Forget about it. Enjoy your stay in the city."

"I'm actually moving here."

"Really?" He looked me up and down and said. "Well, always keep your phone charged at least." He nodded goodbye and walked away.

After another long walk past strange sights and spectrums of people, I ended up at John's and buzzed one more time. After a few seconds a man I don't remember ever meeting opened the door. He had a full head of salt and pepper hair that he kept in a ponytail. He met me with a smile and tired eyes.

"Paul?"

"Yeah, John?"

"Yup. Sorry again about not being here. Something was

wrong with my connection to a client's server and I had to manually reset it. Got home ten minutes before you called."

"It's fine. You're here now. Thank you again."

"No problem." He gestured me to walk in through the doors and continued, "Now that you're here, let me just say in person that I wish you luck in finding what you came for."

Closing the door behind me I said, "Luck and a little bit of help, should be all I need."

CATCHING BUTTERFLIES

THE BRONX WAS ON FIRE and I was watching it burn from my ninth floor window. That's really where it started, since you asked. There were two buildings on the horizon—in Mott Haven probably—that were lighting up the dark sky and otherwise bleak landscape of broken, demolished apartments and abandoned lots. I didn't hear the sirens of fire trucks, and I didn't expect them. That was fine with me though, as the flames were all the distraction I needed from the sounds outside my bedroom door.

I was trying to take my mind off the loud, bilingual noise of my parents as they talked about their disappointment in me. Well, I don't want to be too harsh. They didn't use those words exactly, but that was the gist. I had messed up and they couldn't understand where they went wrong. Why were my grades slipping, and why did the principal have to call in my mom after seeing me tag a hallway with images of butterflies? I certainly didn't have an answer for them. The butterfly thing hadn't become serious yet, only an idea, but I liked the pretty bug and started drawing pictures of it on building steps and in my notebook during class.

My parents went back and forth while I imagined I was a butterfly, able to float through the hot night air to observe the work of efficient arsonists and an overworked fire department which had fifty stations closed by city bureaucrats who looked more at balance sheets than the faces of flesh and blood South Bronx residents. Who knows though? I'm assuming, and this was a long time ago.

"I don't know what else I can do. You can't act like I'm not around. Like I'm not spending time with Danny."

"Not saying that..."

Mumbles. I grabbed my notebook and started drawing. "...but let him understand we're not angry at him."

My parents weren't the volatile type with all that screaming about who fucked up. They talked loudly but with love. As a kid you appreciate that stuff, if only unconsciously. The background conversations and moods of your parents become part of you in an unplanned way, like throwing fertilizer when they think they're just dusting off their hands.

More mumbles, and then, "Okay. Well, I got tomorrow off so what you think about me taking Danny to the park to play some ball and talk?"

"As long as he gets the point that things can't go on like this."

I expected a visit from my dad and within a half hour he knocked on the door of my small room—a partitioned section of the living room. I had positioned my chair to face the window, but when he came in I turned it around to face him and said, "Hey, Daddy."

He didn't smile as he normally did, but he wasn't angry. I assumed he was just tired from working at the warehouse where he tossed boxes of clothes all day.

He said, "You know why I'm here?"

"Cause the principal called Mommy today?"

"Yeah. Me and your mom don't know what's gotten into you lately. Is there something you wanna tell me? Is there a reason why she had to get called?"

What I should have told him was that I wanted to draw but didn't feel like I had any outlets or that anybody cared. Like the kids around the way who painted murals on the ugly brick of half broken buildings, I had something I wanted to express but didn't feel like I had a way of getting it out. Those kids met in the park to dance on cardboard. They played vinyl for the crowds. What I did was draw butterflies cause when I did, I felt like I could fly away from the fires that burned through my borough with all of its wasted potential sucked in by crime and savage economics policies. I wanted others to know that they could fly above it all too.

At ten years old I was, at most, aware of only a quarter of all that. All I could really say was that I was trying to find out who I was. I looked at the floor and said, "I don't know, Daddy."

He sucked on his bottom lip and said, "Tomorrow I'm going to play some ball with Uncle Frank. I want you to come. We can play a little ball and talk little too. How does that sound?"

"That sounds okay."

"Good."

He kissed me on the forehead and lumbered out of the room, leaving me to look forward to the next day. No, of course I didn't really look forward to it. I was never a sports guy. Even now the idea of shooting hoops or swinging a bat are as exciting to me as getting my prostate checked. And as a kid, I could barely stand up against a strong wind.

I eventually heard sirens, but by then the fires had already consumed most of the buildings. Also within sight, though much closer than the fire, was a Friday night party in a neighboring courtyard. With my head turned to the crowd bursting with self-expression, I thought about the bit of vandalism that got me in trouble that day: a butterfly with wings of fire.

The next day the buildings were charred. I kept my eyes on their craggy, charcoal exteriors while slipping into the only T-shirt I had with a team logo. Yankees, of course. I dressed slowly as my father waited for me in the kitchen, finishing breakfast with my mother. After tying my sneakers and kissing mom goodbye we were off to Crotona Park.

I'm not going into how poor the community was. You can find enough stats to tell you what you need in that department. What I remember was that the weather was beautiful. Dad bought me a lemon-flavored piragua from one of the old men who pushed his block of ice and accompanying syrups up and down the block. I remember Dad stopped to joke with a neighbor and they talked shit about what the kids were listening to nowadays.

Most importantly, I remember seeing the 2 train as it sped by. It was covered in spray paint. Every square inch of metal told a story with cartoon characters, stylized letters, and vivid colors that made me stare at each subway car that passed. I'm pretty sure my father noticed me looking, but I can't be one hundred percent about it. Like I said, it was a while ago.

What I wanted to do was run away from the ball court my father was bringing me to and chase that train. I didn't, of course, and walked beside him as we entered the park.

Dad was real athletic with several trophies in the hallway that I never felt too interested in asking about, in the same way I never asked about the gold and white patterned wallpaper. They were both there and in no way connected to any decisions I made. I say that to say that childhood is complicated, right? You want to be yourself or find out what that self is, but you want to feel accepted and loved by those you love. Those desires conflict and you end up not sure where to go. That's how *I* felt anyway, but I'm going to go out on a limb and assume I wasn't the only kid to feel that way.

My uncle Frank was waiting for us at the ball court with his nephew. Frank's Spanish was all kinds of messed up and I would find out a year or so later that he wasn't a blood relation, but a swarthy Italian dude that my father knew from going to school on the north side as a kid. He was funny, and he greeted my dad with a hug.

"Daniel!"

"Hey, Uncle Frank."

"So tell me what's happening? I hear you're trying to redecorate your school?" I looked down with a bashful smile and he told me, "You *should* feel a little bad about it, but I'll leave it to your dad to talk some sense into you. My question is, are you ready to play ball?"

"I think I'm ready."

"Sounds like a champ to me. I'll tell you what." He looked at my father. "For every shot that Daniel and Mike get, I'll get 'em a scoop of ice cream."

"Danny already had a piragua. Too many sweets in one day, Frank."

Uncle Frank turned his head to his nephew who was several feet away. "You hear that, Mike? You need to take some lessons from Daniel and stop eating so much junk."

Dad looked down at me and shook his head at his loud brother from another mother. We walked onto the court and I could hear Frank whisper to my father, "Then he needs to give some lessons to my fucking wife before I need to get a truck to carry her big ass around town." Dad laughed and I sat on the bench next to Mike.

Mike was as tall as me but without my awkward, gangly frame. He moved with a steadiness and strength that was evident even in his relaxed gait. It was the first time I had met him, but after sitting next to him for a combined fifty seconds, I didn't like him. He got up when Uncle Frank waved him in for the beginning of a game with some guys already on the court. Dad sat down in Mike's place.

"So tell me what's been going on?"

"Nothing's going on, Daddy. I messed up, and I promise it won't do it again."

"Why you lying to me, Danny? What made you think that putting marker to your school walls was a good idea in the first place? I don't want to yell at you, but I'm asking cause I want to know. I need to find out if something is wrong so we can fix it."

"I'm not very good at basketball. Not like you."

He craned his neck back with a confused smile and said, "What's that got to do with anything?"

"Sometimes I wish that I was as good as you are."

"Well, you can always practice. If you start practicing a lot now, you could be much better than me when you get older." His eyes opened a little wider, "Is that what you want? To play basketball?"

"I think about it sometimes when I see all those statues on the bookcase. They must mean that people think you're really good."

"I'm a decent player."

I looked on the court to see Mike and Frank playing against the two others. The ease of movement I noticed in the kid my age was even more evident when he played. He handled the ball as if it were attached to his hand by a rubber string, and he was as quick as the flames I watched jumping up and down the night before.

My dad also seemed sucked in and watched along side me until the five-point game ended with Uncle Frank making the last shot. With it done, the other two players left and Uncle Frank shouted to us, "C'mon guys. Mike's trying to get a few scoops of ice cream off me."

It was my turn to move my body and I took to it with all the enthusiasm expected of a chore. I thought about flying away.

Dad seemed happy to get me on the asphalt top next to him and opposite Mike and Uncle Frank. I tried to reciprocate the cheer and smiled as we got ready to start. I breathed in deeply through my teeth and looked at Frank when he raised his eyebrows and asked, "You ready?"

"Yeah."

He nodded, and it began. Frank checked the ball to my father who tried taking it further in court, but Frank was blocking him pretty well. Unable to shake him, Dad forcefully backed into Frank to push him off. He twisted to his right a little and then quickly, and more fully, to his left. He switched hands on the ball and ran past a temporarily disoriented Frank towards the basket. Dad saw Mike break away from me to stop him, but before either he or Frank could reach, Dad jumped up two feet off the ground and let the ball roll off his fingers into the hoop. The whole thing lasted about nine seconds and seemed to impress no one but me.

We got back into formation, but with us now defending the basket on the half court. Dad said, "Daniel, check them the ball." Barely familiar with the language of the sport, I grabbed the ball, inferred what was meant and passed it to Mike, who ran to my right. I showed my lack of coordination for everyone to see when I began flaying my arms, madly trying to stop Mike from throwing the ball or running past me. I hit him high on his right cheek, and after an initial "Ow!" he backed up.

Frank chuckled and said, "Daniel, be careful. I wanna bring him back to my sister the same way I got him."

I tightened my lips in embarrassment. After composing himself Mike took a step backwards away from me and threw the ball directly into the hoop.

The next fifteen minutes were more of the same. They were dunking on me and shooting and passing around me. At one point Dad passed me the ball and told me to take the shot. I missed of course, but Mike and Uncle Frank didn't put up much of an effort to rebound it. I energetically grabbed the ball and tried my luck two more times. I didn't, even once, hit the rim of the basket. I tried to stop them from scoring and failed; I tried to score myself and failed; I tried not to black out from all the running that my body wasn't used to. Only in that did I succeed. Eventually we lost, seven to ten.

Mike and my dad stayed on the court to play two others

who were waiting on the benches for their turn. Uncle Frank and I both headed to our own spot on the sidelines as they played. Uncle Frank said, "If your father wants to play again, let him. My energy ran out five minutes ago." He guzzled from a nearby fountain, sat on the bench, and leaned back until he was looking at the sky right above the park's tree line.

I looked away and back to my father who continued to play as we rested. Having already embarrassed myself, I got over it a little and just looked at the four of them battle it out on the court.

Because I wasn't very good at sports, I'd never shown any interest in watching my dad play, but he was amazing. It hurt me a little. You don't understand. He was *already* this large figure. He fixed whatever was broken around the apartment with a smile. Everyone in the neighborhood liked him. He came in tired from work almost every day, but always had enough energy to knock on my door before going to sleep just to talk to me or ask what I learned in school. I wondered if I would be like him. Could I be like him? Or should I not even think in those terms?

My dad walked off the court and pulled Uncle Frank up from the bench as he said with a laugh, "Get your ass up there." He sat down and smiled at me. "How do you think our game went?"

I looked down with a smile again and replied, "I think I need more practice."

"Do you want more practice?"

I looked back up and with wide eyes said, "You were great up there."

"That was me. I asked about you, Danny. Do you wanna want to practice more?"

I didn't respond. Dad put his arm around my neck, pulled me closer, and kissed my forehead. The sweat from his chin dripped onto my nose, but I didn't mind.

"The things I do, I do because that is what makes me feel good. *I* like coming to the park to play, but that's not for everyone. Your mother, you know, she likes the knitting thing. You have to do what *you* like. Do what's right for you." He was contemplative for a moment then said, "What if I buy you a book you can draw in? Maybe even get you a few canvases or something we can put in the living room for you to paint on? Would you like that instead of the school walls?"

"Can you afford to get that stuff?"

"Don't think about that. I'm just asking if that is what you want to do."

"Yeah. I think so."

"Okay then. I'll get those things for you in a few weeks." With his arm around me he squeezed me closer to him. "Why don't you go get your notebook, come back here, and you can draw while me and your uncle Frank play ball?"

I nodded and ran back to my apartment to do just that. I sat on the grass next to the court and drew the rest of that day.

Dad did what he said he would and it had the desired effect of keeping me out of trouble. As I got older I moved on to writing, what the newspapers called graffiti, until two things happened. I got into a gallery, and then a short while after that a friend of mine died while we were tagging a billboard. I realized that if I kept writing, I'd end up with my parents picking me up at a police station or a morgue. Right before my friend died, though I got into a gallery. This is when being a writer started to get attention outside of the neighborhood. Eventually, I got an agent, I sold a piece, and the rest is history. That answer your question?

THE CIRCUS

HE STARED AT HER BREASTS as he talked. At first, Catherine thought it was flattering, so she maintained her smile as he spoke about that funny moment when he realized that all of the men in his office were gay. He said, "Not that there's anything wrong with that, but at some point, I have to start wondering, why haven't any of these guys hit on me yet? You know? It makes me feel a little inadequate that I'm not worth at least a glance."

She laughed, he laughed, they ate vegetarian noodles. Throughout dinner, however, his eyes never lost their carnivorous focus on her chest. Soon the attention lost its charm and turned from flattering to rude to then downright creepy.

The date that had its beginnings two days before when Catherine give her number to a guy she met at a friend's party. It ended with an awkward goodbye outside a Thai restaurant as he moved in for a hug that she knew he would turn into a cheap feel. She shook his hand instead and nodded slightly when he said, "Maybe we can meet again this weekend?" Catherine unclenched her jaw and responded, "Maybe. I'll text you later when I know what I'm doing."

He turned around to climb into a waiting cab and her muscles slowly relaxed. The uncomfortable tension that came with being looked at as a thing was easing its way through her pores like a toxin she had to sweat out. She watched him as he got inside the cab and, as if his skull were made of glass, Catherine could see the lubricated fantasies that filled his head.

Standing there, after her sixth first date in three months, a headshake was all Catherine could muster as she tried to avoid the rain beyond the restaurant's front awning. She was doing a lazy job of it, and by the time she got inside a cab, raindrops were trickling down her cheeks and chin. Catherine wondered why she was even out there. What was the use?

Catherine watched Helen as she checked out her reflection in the mirrored wall. Helen had changed sweaters right after they left the office that day and she wanted to make sure her makeup was still presentable. After Helen confirmed that her face was on properly, Catherine watched her self-inspection turn to vain admiration as she looked at her own shapely, but wide, body. Examining the curves of her hips, Helen said, "Yeah, I know. But I wanted us to at least give this thing a try."

Catherine sat back on the faux leather couch and stared at the ceiling tiles. Her eyes were working their way out of the maze made by patterns above her head. She found herself at an impasse and said, "I guess. Still. I could've stayed in the office. That blouse we were working on has to be ready by Monday, and I'm pretty sure I won't even find Mr. Adequate, let alone Mr. Right, speed dating in a lounge called Pounders."

Helen said, "Maybe, maybe not. But I'm pretty sure you'll find a guy who won't look at your tits like he's planning on eating them with fava beans and a nice chianti."

Catherine's loud, high-pitched laughter turned the heads of the other women in the room. They each sat on their own faux leather or faux suede seat, waiting for instructions from Regina, the woman who was organizing the event.

Earlier Catherine had maneuvered her way through the red-stained toilet paper perils of the lounge's female restroom. After hovering above a filthy toilet, she saw Regina on her way out. Catherine recognized her from her website and again as she stepped into the ladies' lounge area. Regina had presumably just finished talking to the men in the adjoining room. The thirty-somethings were all forced to mingle within same-sex groups as they waited anxiously for something exciting, or at least something different, to happen.

The men wondered what the women looked like. The women wondered about everything else. Though it didn't seem likely, Catherine asked herself if she would find someone special. She stared again at the ceiling and tried to express, at least to herself, what exactly she was looking for. Her recent string of failed dates put into focus the fact that Catherine wasn't sure what that was. Though in the time it took Helen to go to the bar and return with a martini, she had come up with an answer.

It was simple, Catherine thought. She wanted a connection. She wanted moments when you realize that the person you're with knows precisely how you feel about things said and unsaid because they feel it too. She wanted to spend lazy Saturdays in bed with a loving man who laughed at reality TV right along with her. She wanted someone who encouraged her to be open and creative in ways she would be afraid to otherwise. Catherine just wanted someone who understood her.

She told her friend as much. In response, Helen sucked her teeth and sipped her apple martini, draped in an aura of jaded cynicism. Helen said she was looking for a Spanish guy with a sense of humor and a thing for chubby white girls.

Regina entered the ladies' waiting area wearing a beautiful lavender outfit and a smile that, to Catherine, seemed too bright to be real. Regina's skirt suit fit her hourglass form perfectly and impressed the women in the room who looked on with subtle envy or attraction. Regina's skin was flawless chocolate, and the expert weave she used to cover her real hair was almost undetectable. Except for her large green eyes, Regina's facial features were small and cute— like an erotic cartoon. It made Catherine think about the slight stretch marks that crept a centimeter or so above the coverage of her D-cup bra.

Catherine began dwelling on her other imperfections as Regina warmly introduced herself and spoke to the group about their next steps in finding the love of their life. "Hello, ladies! So, first off, I'm Regina. I spoke to all of you over the phone or through email, and I'm happy to see that we have such a great turnout. Welcome to all of you!"

Catherine thought of the dull and uneven brown skin

that covered her body. Examining the lifeless Catherine mannequin in her mind while looking at Regina, she could see laugh lines that seemed as broad as canyons.

Regina went on, "You're all just gorgeous today!" The women demurely moved their bodies in reflexive reaction to the compliment, but Catherine thought about the slight indentation in her back left thigh. It looked like a cellulite dimple, but it was actually the mark of a childhood accident where she'd fallen on a wire fence. A passing comment from a long-ago ex turned it from a forgotten scar to another thing she obsessed about.

Regina continued, "I'm sure I'll be saying the same thing to the men. I did my best to find ones who matched what you ladies were looking for, and I think you'll all be pleasantly surprised by who you'll be meeting in the next few minutes."

Catherine listened intently but also thought about her thigh hole, her hair, her ass, and her stomach while she heard Regina tell the women in the dimly lit room the procedures they were expected to follow. They would eventually sit in front of the men who were waiting patiently in the other dimly lit room. Chairs and tables were set up in the larger, main lounge area so that the men and women could face each other with three minutes to talk. A timer would go off, and the men would rotate, while the women remained seated.

Regina gave them suggestions on what introductory questions to ask, and by the time Helen had finished her martini, it was time to meet the complete strangers in the next room.

Everyone rose from their seats and followed Regina through the doorway and into the ample space. Catherine wondered how much Regina paid to rent the spot, but her estimate dropped by a few hundred dollars when she saw Regina flirting with Rex, the owner of Pounders. He charmlessly sidled next to Regina while also eye groping Catherine and every other woman who was there.

Catherine noticed Rex as she walked by him to get to her table. He had a face like a frog, breath like a dragon, and long, matted, gray-black hair like a jungle sloth. Rex stood with an expensive camera to take pictures of the event for the lounge's website. Regina winked at him in what Catherine assumed was a game to help her bargain down the price. Rex winked right back with a smirk as Regina sat the women down on one side of a row of closely arranged tables. When they were all seated, she went to get the men.

From what Catherine saw, they weren't at all disappointing physically. There were two awkward exceptions, but as a whole, the fifteen men were attractive. Helen thought the same and whispered, "Oooo, shit. These guys are sexy!"

Regina sat the men in their assigned seats. She made a few cheerful statements about relaxing and having fun, and then rang a buzzer and told everyone to start talking before time ran out.

Catherine made a quick assessment of the man across from her: he wore a gray blazer and a light blue T-shirt that almost perfectly matched the color of his eyes. His jet-black hair was cut close, and his perfectly shaped jawline and cheekbones reminded her of a superhero in their exaggerated masculinity. Catherine said, "Hi."

Sounding as excited and nervous as Catherine was, he replied, "Hi. My name's Jonathan."

"Catherine." She paused for a moment then said, "Can I be honest Jonathan?"

ALEX CLERMONT

He nodded his head cautiously and said, "Please."

"I'm very glad you're sitting in front of me right now."

They both laughed, though hers lessened slightly when she heard his. He laughed in sinister sounding yelps that surprised Catherine in a way she tried not to show on her face for fear of embarrassing him.

"Me too." He said, "I mean, I hate sounding superficial," his eyes quickly scanned her face, "but you're breathtaking."

"Thank you. Wow." She said with a wide grin, forgetting about his laugh.

"What? Did I say something wrong?"

"No. It's just that you seemed so sincere when you said it. Plus, men usually say words like sexy instead of breathtaking."

"I'm sincere most of the time," he said. Catherine laughed as he talked on. "Plus, I don't like using words that boil women down to just sex."

"Wow, again," Catherine said. "So, Jonathan, why did you decide to do this? Speed dating, I mean."

"Well, I just came off a bad break up a few months ago, and I saw this as a good way to put myself out there again—succeed or fail. Who knows? And you? What are you looking for?"

"I'm guessing the same thing we all want. Just someone to spend time with. Hoping something long term comes from it, but I'm just going with the flow for today. I've had a lot of bizarre first dates recently, so a friend and I wanted to give this a chance before we gave up dating completely and just got a bunch of cats."

Jonathan chuckled, but his eyes stayed on Catherine's face. She felt her cheeks warm up, but then she noticed a thin rope that hung around his neck, underneath his shirt.

Without thinking, she asked, "What's that?"

Jonathan followed her line of sight and said, "This?" as he pulled out an intricately carved wooden cross hanging from the rope. "It's just a reminder."

"What of?" she asked.

"My dedication to our Lord, Jesus Christ."

"Oh. Okay. So you're really religious."

"That's kind of a relative term, I think. I just try my best to live as our Lord did. I attend worship services as often as I can, and I try to live in accordance with His word."

Catherine looked as upbeat as before but began to mentally countdown the time left until the buzzer would go off. She guessed that she had fifteen seconds.

"Have you accepted Jesus Christ as your savior?"

"Uh…maybe we can talk about that later." The buzzer buzzed and soon another man was sitting in front of Catherine. Less enthusiastic than before she said, "Hi."

He said, "Hello. My name's Albert. And you?"

"Catherine. Nice to meet you, Albert. Is that an accent I hear in your voice?"

"A slight one." He flashed a coy grin. His light brown eyes contrasted the darkness of his skin. In the second that Catherine took all this in, she also noticed his muscular body. She imagined her ankles wrapped around his waist while he effortlessly lifted her naked body off some plush hotel bed to stroke her against a wall.

Albert said, "I was raised in Jamaica until I was ten."

Catherine's eyes opened wide. "That place looks so beautiful…I mean from the commercials." She felt a little embarrassed by her tourist's view of his home country, but Albert just said, "It is."

"I love your locks, by the way."

"Thanks. I got them when I was eighteen, mainly for fashion. I've been thinking of cutting them though. I'm getting a few too many stares at my new job."

She asked, "What do you do?"

"I'm a corporate accounts manager at one of the more unpopular banks."

"You mean mine?"

He chuckled then said, "I like what you're doing with your hair. It looks great."

"Really? Some guys don't really dig the natural look."

"You pull it off very well. Like you put time into styling it."

"Thank you for saying that."

"You're more than welcome, Catherine." He then said, "So this seems to be going pretty well." She looked away shyly as he grinned. "If you always wanted to go to Jamaica, well, I go every summer. Even got a place there. If things work out between us, maybe we can go together."

"I'll definitely keep the invitation in mind. Tell me about the country. All I know is from TV ads and co-opted Bob Marley songs."

"I can't tell you too much in the minute we have left, but what I love is that the people there seem more authentic, and what's right and wrong is more easily understood. Unlike this country sometimes, where everything is so gray."

Catherine furrowed her brow a little and asked, "What do you mean?"

"Well, like, I grew up in a traditional household. The way I was raised, the man takes the lead. He's the head of the household. I think that's the natural order of things."

"Can you give me an example of 'taking the lead'?" Catherine said, her narrowing eyelids giving her a suspicious look.

"For example," Albert continued, his tone changed to match Catherine's expression, "If a husband makes enough to support him and his wife, she shouldn't be working. His job is to support them financially. Her job is to support the family."

"I'm a clothing designer. I like my job. I don't think I should have to leave it if my husband says I should."

Albert was about to speak but closed his mouth instead while smiling uncomfortably. They were silent for five seconds and then the buzzer went off.

Another man sat in front of Catherine, then another, and another. Each three-minute chunk that passed took with it just a little bit more of her energy as clichés for undateable men sat in front of her. One guy was a subtle racist. After him, was a man who lived with his parents and had no desire to change that. The last man she saw was one of the two who stood out for the wrong reasons. His huge eyes and short face reminded her of Rex, who she saw taking photos and chatting up a genial, but naturally reluctant, Regina.

Right before the buzzer timed out on Rex's doppelgänger, he leaned across the table towards a surprised Catherine for a hug. Rex jumped from the background and took a photo of the two before Catherine's face could reflect what she was thinking—creating a picture of what looked like pleasant confusion instead of surprise and slight anger. As the bright spots faded from Catherine's vision, the look-a-like got up and walked towards the bar along with everyone else who was either already getting a drink or getting out of their seat to do so.

When Catherine's eyes eventually cleared themselves of the flashing bright lights, she could see people mingling at the bar. They paired off in free-floating couples. Occasionally they'd switch partners with another couple in subtle movements that seemed as flawless as practiced dance steps.

She glanced around and saw Helen smiling while lightly touching the arm of one of the fifteen men.

When he had sat down in front of Catherine earlier, she'd guessed that he was Hispanic. Remembering Helen's preference, she was almost sure of it now. They were getting drinks, and he would sneak a glimpse of Helen's ass whenever their eyes weren't meeting. Catherine smirked at the scene as she got up, ready to get her things and go home.

The last forty-five minutes confirmed for her that she should not have been there. She wasn't sure where she should have been, but the rush to find out was now gone. She wondered when would be the best time to go to the pet store and get that cat. After breakfast, she figured—after breakfast tomorrow.

With Catherine not participating in the bar-side pairing, the group of men and women were in constant, frenetic motion. Some single man seeking a partner would intrude in on a couple and force that man to find another woman. Catherine went to the bar, to space not occupied by the jostling beehive of activity. She waited until a bartender was free and said, "Johnnie Walker Black, please."

He brought it quickly, and she drank it even quicker. She paid and walked towards the door when she noticed Regina, from the corner of her eye, being talked at by Rex. Regina politely nudged Rex away and caught Catherine before her hand reached the doorknob.

"You're not leaving yet are you?" Regina asked.

"Yeah, I didn't find anything here worth staying for. Not

to blame you, of course, but there just wasn't a match."

"Really? After our conversation last week, I figured you and Leonard would really hit it off."

"He's a bit too testosterone-y for me." She said, looking over Regina's shoulder at Helen's new guy friend. As Helen bent her neck to drink her third martini, he snuck another look at her ass through her tight skirt. "Plus, I don't think I'm his type." She looked back at Regina. "Tonight just made me realize how much I'm not meant for this kind of stuff."

Regina tried not to crack the pleasant facade of interest she would need when going back to Rex, but she looked at Catherine as if searching for an answer.

"Dating, I mean. It's just too much…energy, time, emotions. And for what? I mean every boyfriend I've ever had either dumped me or got dumped by me. All that time I could've started my own clothing label. I could've traveled the world. I could've started a new career as a lion tamer or a Guinness record holder for the world's longest toenail." Regina laughed. "Why? Why keep doing this?" Catherine asked.

Regina pursed her lips and tilted her head slightly before she said, "Because as corny as it sounds, everybody needs somebody."

"You may be right, but tomorrow I'm getting a cat." Regina laughed, and Catherine said with a smirk, "I hope everyone else here has better luck than I did."

"Goodbye, Catherine."

Catherine walked onto the Columbus Avenue sidewalk to hail a cab. One came speeding down the street, but as she got herself ready to jump inside, it passed her by and stopped a dozen or so feet away near a man who had also been waiting on the curb. He opened the door, but before his feet got off the ground, he saw Catherine, who was looking at the cab with a disappointed frown on her face.

"Hey," he said in a raised voice. "If you want it, you got it. I'm in no rush."

Catherine walked over, intending to take him up on his offer, but instead said, "Maybe we can split it. Where are you heading?"

From the front seat, the cab driver interrupted them by shouting, "My friend, either you come in, or you close the door."

"Heading to Brooklyn," he said to Catherine, ignoring the driver.

"Well, me too. Come on," Catherine said as she jumped into the back seat through the door that he held open. He followed suit, and with both of them inside, the driver sped off.

Catherine looked out of the window. The evening lights of the city were turning on as the late sunset faded away. The emerging indigo sky was beautiful, and she stared at the colors while daydreaming about nothing.

Was there something wrong with her that she just couldn't see? Are her standards that much higher than everyone else's? What woman was dating the chauvinist or the missionary? Those two men, and every other man that night who was rotated around like sushi on a conveyor belt at a Midtown all-you-can-eat, would find someone who fit them like a glove. They'd lay in bed, in bliss or in prayer, with their better half, and one day get married while Catherine would merely get old.

Those thoughts made her as sad as she was on her last first date—until she stopped feeling sad. Catherine knew that there was nothing wrong with her, at least nothing more than the inherited frailties that came with being alive. Her standards were high because she deserved more than what she saw that night.

Catherine gave herself a pat on the back as she turned her gaze to the people on the sidewalks flying past her backseat window. Fuck those guys, she thought. I'm okay without them.

She paid no attention to the man sitting next to her until he eventually said, "What part of Brooklyn do you live in?"

"Why?"

"Cause the cab is going to cross the bridge eventually. When we get there, he should know where to go first."

"I'm in Bedford Hills."

"Oh okay. I'm in Clinton Hill, so I guess I'll go first."

Catherine nodded and turned her head to look out of the window again. She turned back when he asked, "Don't you mean Bedford-Stuyvesant?"

"Yeah, but the proper name of the part I live in is Bedford Hills. Are you from New York?"

"Absolutely." Catherine looked on in silence. "I recently came back from being overseas for a few years, though I actually grew up in Bed-Stuy. It was a lot rougher when I was growing up there though."

"Overseas?" She said, "Are you in the military?"

"No, I worked for an architectural firm that moved to Germany. They offered a nice relocation package, so I left. But after a while, I just missed being home."

"You missed Bed-Stuy?" Catherine said.

"In a way. I missed that warm feeling you get when you're somewhere familiar—a place that has..." His eyes seemed to lose focus, but he continued, "I missed seeing and talking to people who understand me and what I feel, without me having to explain it to death. I was tired of being in a room full of strangers." Regaining focus and looking Catherine in the eyes, he said, "You know what I mean?"

"I understand exactly what you mean."

There was a comfortable pause between them until he eventually said, "I also missed my cat."

She chuckled, and then asked, "You left your cat here?"

"Well, my parent's cat. I got it for them a few years before I left to stave off their eventual divorce. He's a cute, fat Russian Blue named Buddha who moves as slow and as funny as you'd think a fat cat would." Catherine laughed as she pictured the grown man across from her running after the comical pet like a toddler.

"By the way, my name's Gary."

Catherine looked at Gary's genuine smile and outstretched hand. She sighed in surrender and shook it. "My name's Catherine."

"Do you have a pet, Catherine?"

"I was thinking about getting one tomorrow actually, but I'm not sure anymore. I may be a little too busy."

BUILDINGS OF CLAY

IN MY MIND, Mr. Yang was a kind of math god—an Asian Zeus who threw blindingly bright long division questions instead of lightning bolts. He was handsome, six feet two inches tall and towered above the rest of us mere mortals at the front of the class without a smile on his face or a wrinkle in whatever suit he had on. Aside from his height, Mr. Yang also stood out from the school full of dingy polo shirt-wearing teachers because he was able to answer any question put to him in a way that impressed those in the room who understood the problem in the first place.

The whole thing was too intimidating for words, and for the last three months—every morning at second-period—intimidated was exactly how I felt. My problem was that I just wanted to drop out—to run away from that building and its math classes—but instead, I sat in the chair farthest from Mr. Yang's desk and transformed from a blood-and-bone seventeen-year-old to a kind of jelly creature while he prepared us for the upcoming statewide math tests. The results would determine how much money our school would get, which teachers would get fired, and what direction our lives would take. With probably ninety percent of us aware of what was at stake I would say that 89.9 percent of my class, including me, tried to wish it all away.

I wanted to wake up one day and hear that the president announced some national emergency, indefinitely postponing all standardized testing. I'd go to college, get a job, and whenever my co-workers and I would talk about our high school days at the local bar they'd hear me tell them with nostalgic reverence the same old story: "You remember that alien invasion we had ten years ago? Well, I didn't have to take the statewide math tests because of it. They just let us go to the next grade." I'd smile and drink my beer down to the dregs.

The fantasy floated around in my mind as I sat in first-period earth science. I would take up class time filling in the dream's different variables and try to put flesh on the illusion. What kind of beer would I be drinking? What kind of job would I have? I decided that the answer for both was microbrew. I knew it was a fantasy though. My beerless reality involved me digging in my nose and daydreaming.

My thoughts shifted between Mr. Yang, invading aliens, and Mrs. Liatris's breasts. I watched as they came dangerously close to popping out of her tube-top dress when she leaned over to pick up transparency slides that explained the mechanics of volcanism. As usual, her tits threatened to reveal themselves but never followed through. I remained unmoved. Next period was math, and even Mrs. Liatris's perfectly shaped C-cups couldn't change my mood, to say nothing of algebra.

I got up with the bell's first ring and slowly walked out the door. I thought about a little acceptance letter in my book bag when I saw Hendricks standing across the classroom entrance, leaning against the dull, gray-green lockers that lined the hallways. When he saw me, Hendricks let his skateboard drop and then gave me the handshake.

"Mayor of the LES. What's the haps, Mr. Hendricks?"

"Nothing at all. What's going on with you, porn star?"

I smiled at the new nickname. Every few weeks for the last two years he dug into his bottomless bag of nouns to find a word to put in front of "star." He did it because he thought it was clever. He was right.

"What happened to 'track star'?" I asked.

"That was the Jason of last month. You're not gonna run away anymore, so that dude is dead and gone. You're here now, and all is as it should be."

"Was that deep?"

"If it was, it wouldn't matter. We in school, ain't we?"

He gave a long exhale and then picked his Afro with a big-toothed comb that he kept in his back pocket. As far as best friends went, Hendricks had almost all the attributes you'd want. He liked Spider-man over Superman; he listened when I talked; his occasional jokes never had the quality of being backhanded insults that took you a minute or so to get angry about—a rarity in the sardonic apathy that filled Thomas Paine High School.

Hendricks asked, "Who you got now?"

"Mr. Yang."

"Ah. Your archnemesis." He chuckled.

"Cut that shit out."

"You always have something to say about that guy. I

figured you would ace his class. You two being peoples and all that."

"You think he's gonna give me a cheat sheet because we both share an epithelial fold? Forget that, man." Hendricks laughed, but with no trace of playfulness I continued, "I'm serious. There's nothing funny about this. I'm getting hit with a bunch of numbers and formulas that always get more complicated. I hate that class." His smile mellowed as he listened to the beginnings of my rant. "But it's not only math. That's the point of the knife, but it's also history, English, and...and...dude, I'm so tired of coming here. I'm failing most of my classes, and if you asked me, I couldn't tell you why. I mean, I'm relatively smart, I know that much, but it's like my brain shuts down when I walk through these doors, and I can't keep all the words they dump on me from piling up into a mess in my mind." My voice lowered. I looked away and said, "I think I might drop out."

Hendricks scrutinized my face during a dramatic pause, then said, "Come on. Let's go outside. We got another fifteen minutes till class starts."

He stepped hard on the back of his board, making the front jump to his hand. Hendricks picked it up and, carrying it under his right arm, walked beside me as we headed toward one of the dozens of unlocked exits that we always seemed to find. High school was just a shitty jail. The imposing doors were incompetently guarded, and nothing kept you inside besides your desire to not piss off your parents.

That fear of adults had disappeared, at least for the next few minutes, and so we sat near some crumbling concrete steps outside, near a metal side door. I pulled out a cigarette and lit up as Hendricks sat on his board with his back against the wall. The sky was mostly clear, but between pulls

I watched as the fuzzy shadows cast by the occasional cloud, darkened whatever was unfortunate enough to be under them. The shadows never hit us though, and so the diffused light from the sunrise continually shine on us.

That yellowy-gold color tinted everything for seconds at a time, so when I glanced at Hendricks light was shimmering off his face in a way that made him look like a bronze statue. I exhaled and wondered what kind of precious metal I would be made from if someone caught a glimpse of me standing in the sunlight for longer than the two seconds of an attendance check.

"So were you serious in there?" Hendricks asked, "You thinking about dropping out?"

"Yeah, I am."

"Okay. So talk. What exactly is the problem?"

"I told you before that I don't know what's going on. My brain just won't function right in there."

"Try to explain. Humor me."

I shook my head slightly and tried to think of what my first word should be. "Classes." I stopped then, "Classes about dead men who discovered something that no one's cared about in years. Some white guys killed some not-white guys. Solving mathematic matrices and other abstract shit that will mean just as much nothing to me twenty years from now as it does today. I mean, why the hell should I care about any of this stuff?" Hendricks let out a low chuckle as I emphasized hell. I smirked, paused to knock the ash off the tip of my cigarette, and then continued, "I can't remember the last time I heard my dad—or anyone's dad— talk about Bacon's Rebellion. We're told so much, and it's so damn unimportant and overwhelming at the same time.

"What really scares me is that I'm supposed to go through

college after this. I think about it, and I shiver inside, man. Years of tests. Of cramming and trying to memorize stuff I forget the next day. Waking up early to be told every few months how much better everyone else is when the grades come in…"

I took the last pull from my cigarette and tossed the butt. "I want to get a job now. Skip all that. Be a plumber or something."

"Is this what's been getting to you the last couple of days?"

"Mainly, yeah. I've applied to a few trade schools." Hendricks waited for me to continue. "I got accepted to one that might have me working on air conditioners or something like that. Been walking around with their letter in my bag since last Tuesday, but I'm still not a hundred percent about it."

Hendricks said, "Well, I wish I had some real advice for you. Some magic words that would change everything."

"I wish you did too, Mr. Mayor."

"I can only advise that you relax."

"Uh huh." I nodded dismissively.

"No, I'm real here, Jason. You've got like what? Another semester till you have to think about college and the stuff after high school? Maybe you'll go, maybe you won't, but this stuff isn't so hard that you can't at least graduate. And graduating here may mean more in the long run than from a place where you work on air conditioners."

"I'm not…"

He interrupted. "Not that there's anything wrong with that." I looked at him, and he shrugged his shoulders. "I'm just saying."

"Look, it's not that it's hard. I just can't take it in there."

"What is 'there'?"

"Are you shitting me? What are we talking about? School."

"It's a building. It's just a pretty box. Life is the stuff that happens outside of it. Cram and test for two more semesters and you're done with it. High school's not that drastic, porn star. You can fake it until you get an idea of what your options are and what you want to do. Running from this place to another one just like it won't solve your problems. It might even create new ones."

"Well said. Is that it?"

"That's all I have to give, man. You can get through this, and you don't need me to tell you anything else but that."

Hendricks got up and dusted the skateboard dirt off his ass. I took the advice for what it was worth. With the last few minutes we had left between classes, we walked to the bodega. On the way there, I stared at graffitied brick walls that I had seen and marveled at a million times before. The painting was of a crack in the brick that revealed a world inside that was greener and better than ours. It had bluer skies and fields of flowers, whereas I had nothing but piss-stained concrete sidewalks to walk on.

We continued to the corner store where I bought some grape soda, and Hendricks got a pack of sour cream and onion potato chips that made his breath smell like rot. He chewed his last mouthful as we got ready to walk into school. I told him, "Your breath smells like old kitchen garbage."

"You should smell it after I eat...*yo mama.*"

"Fuck you, man." I laughed.

As we entered the building, my laughter died down, and our smiles disappeared. We moved at a funereal pace towards our respective classes. Before making a left, I said, "See you in a few, Mr. Hendricks."

He replied, "See you later, porn star," as he continued ahead.

Thin, straight lines of sun pierced through the thick glass and safety bars of the hallway windows, but they were never enough. Even at 8:55 in the morning the fluorescent lights were on and overpowered anything the natural world could produce.

In here, I had to pass a statewide test. Then I'd have to pass the next one. I'd have to cram for class exams and smaller quizzes too. It was a hamster wheel, and everyone was running in it. Mr. Johnson even half-joked in class last week that he needed us to pass the coming English tests or he'd be on the unemployment line, begging for a job, and eating mayonnaise sandwiches. We all laughed, but it was the same kind of laughter that comes with hearing someone's dog is in the veterinary ER for eating a bag of Kit Kats: the situation sounded hilariously implausible and sad at the same time.

I got to class and fell into my seat next to the door. Mr. Yang was sitting silently at his desk, grading quizzes from another class. His eyes were focused and moved left to right without pause. This class was the most massive stone in the wall that I banged my head against every Monday through Friday. I assumed Mr. Yang knew that, though I also assumed that I was too small for him to care.

A few seconds after I sat down he looked at his watch and stood up. The moment his back was erect, the bell rang, and I shook my head at the clockwork precision. Was he a part of the school or was the machinery of the bell system a part of him?

Feeling tired already, I closed my eyes halfway and slumped low in my chair. My metamorphosis into a jelly creature was about to begin.

Mr. Yang said, "Good morning. If you've been paying attention to the syllabus, then you know that today we're going to take a break from our normal class structure." A few of us looked around for answers. Someone muttered, "Huh?"

Mr. Yang continued in the same bland voice, "If you haven't been following the syllabus that I gave everyone here on the first and second day of class, then know that for the next two classes I'm going to talk to each of you individually about your performance in this class thus far—including weaknesses, strengths, and strategies for turning your weaknesses into strengths."

We stopped looking around and, in our own unique ways, tried to hide while sitting in plain sight. I put my down on the table and behind my folded arms. Next to me, Steve sat perfectly still—not even blinking—in what I guessed was an attempt to blend into the background like a camouflaged praying mantis.

Mr. Yang continued, "I'll talk to each of you, one-on-one, outside while the rest of your classmates busy themselves quietly. You can think of it as a free period, but I suggest you study yesterday's notes concerning the outline of the upcoming statewide math test. You'll come outside in alphabetical order. The student I finish talking to will let the next student know to meet me outside."

I got a little nervous as he called Deirdre Aaron. My Jason Ahn trumped any of the other names in class. They both walked past me and I thought, what, exactly, is he going to tell Deirdre? As Mr. Yang closed the door behind them though, I thought, what the hell is he going to tell *me*? I began to imagine him pulling out old classwork of mine from last semester to kindergarten. Maybe even that quiz I took the year before and fell asleep on top of—the lightly browned edges of my dried drool stain forever marking my wrong answers.

I kept being told by teachers that I'd better study for the next test, do the homework, pay attention to the lesson. I tried at first—I mean I tried to try—but I always gave up. Like a cooking pot, they kept pouring facts into my head until it just overflowed. I could only take so much before I tuned out.

I looked at the other kids as they talked or read books at their desk. Some were nodding off as they waited for their name to be next. I wondered if I was the only one to feel so out of place. Was I the only one who felt that things were so big and stupid? Maybe I was, and maybe Mr. Yang was going to tell me that. With every math test I've ever taken in his hand, he'd say that I was an idiot destined to deliver pizzas until my back became bent from old age. I'd end up a hunched-over senior citizen performing manual labor to make up for what social security didn't provide.

I imagined long division lightning bolts shooting from his eyes.

Deirdre came in and tapped me on the right shoulder. I jumped in my seat at the touch, and she said, "You're next, Jay." I got up and walked to the door. I prepared to have my future told to me, and to respond by dropping out to fix air conditioners tomorrow.

In the hallway, Mr. Yang was sitting behind a small desk that had been dragged out of the classroom. His head was down, and his back was to me as he looked over some papers. Without turning, he said, "Please sit down, Jason." I did so without a peep. He looked up from his papers and sniffed the air. Looking me in the face, he said, "You smell like cigarette smoke, Jason."

My eyes darted around a bit as I avoided responding. He continued, "It's a bad habit, especially for someone your age. I would suggest you stop." I quietly agreed. "Well, we don't have too much time, but before I go over my assessment, I'd like to hear your opinion on how well you think you're doing in my class, and what you think you need help in."

"I, uh, I don't know. I mean, honestly, I don't think I'm doing anything right. I do the homework, but I don't understand all of it. Not even well enough to ask questions. I study, but I never remember any of it when I have to take the test. I was never really good at math, and I leave every class feeling defeated. I don't know what else to say. That's it."

He looked me in the eyes for a silent second or two, and I could feel my bladder weaken a bit. He eventually said, "Jason, I would suggest that you take advantage of the math tutoring program. We're one of a handful of public schools in the city able to sustain such a thing. You'll get individual attention, and pick up better study habits. As for your feelings, I think you should go to the guidance counselor. You're too young to feel defeated by anything, and they can certainly give you better advice than I could about how to overcome that." I nodded in quiet agreement.

"Okay. So let's take a look at some of your specific issues from class. Things you can expand on later." He shuffled through the papers in front of him. Then without any facial expressions to warn me, Mr. Yang farted. Mr. Yang farted loudly. His eyes opened wide in surprise, and he said, "Sorry, Jason. Excuse me." After a moment he said, "That was pretty embarrassing." I wasn't sure whether to laugh or be disgusted. I did neither, and after a few seconds, he excused himself again and then continued to talk math.

He brought up a couple of my past tests and let me know the patterns he noticed. He made a few suggestions, and I listened. Some of what he said was crap, much of it was really helpful, and the rest I didn't understand, though I nodded as if I did. He told me to try to set learning goals for the next few days until the test. I agreed that I would and at the same time wondered if the smell would hit me. I thought I caught a whiff of something, but it was too subtle for me to be sure. He finished without another mention of it.

When I got up, he said, "Please tell Derrick to come out."

"All right."

I went back inside and watched Derrick nervously walk out after I let him know that he was next. For all his perfect enunciations and professional appearance, Mr. Yang was human. Being gross made him especially human, and I allowed the corners of my mouth to rise a little.

His advice was decent too. The combination made things seem easier than they were ten minutes ago. A stupid test was just that, and there was no such thing as a math god. Not much had changed, but I felt a weight lifted off my chest as I realized that everything was manageable. I'd continue to get graded, maybe I'd do worse on some days than others, but there would be more days and more chances, and I could do it.

I opened the math book to go over some of Mr. Yang's suggestions. I thought about passing the statewide but knew that if I didn't, I'd be fine. Life would continue, inside and outside of this place.

SOFT

Peter never imagined that bare knuckles alone could cause so much ruin to the human face. He'd seen plenty of violent TV shows and action movies, but had only a faint idea of the ugliness that a really strong punch created—he once saw the puffy, closed right eye of an MMA fighter while channel surfing on a Sunday night. What he was looking at now, however, was something entirely different. It was Karen who had been hit. It was he who'd hit her. In the dim, afternoon light of his bedroom Peter saw with vivid detail what a punch could do, and there was no suited announcer to separate him from the reality of the scene.

He stared at Karen as she lay on the floor, remorseful and crying, and he could see the skin on her cheek was torn slightly by the force and friction of his fist. She swelled right before his eyes. With each second her jaw filled with fluids that caused a sad looking asymmetry in the face of the girl Peter said he loved. She whimpered, "I'm sorry" over and over again as tears fell down her face and mucus from her nose ran into her mouth.

He hit her out of reflex more than anything else.

Earlier the two had been in Peter's bed. With his parents out of town for the weekend, they indulged in awkward teenage sex. Still figuring out the contours of their own bodies, Karen and Peter kissed and rubbed in out-of-sync rhythms that they weren't old enough to feel embarrassed about. Energy spent, they giggled without much self-reflection and lost themselves in Peter's sheets, panting.

After a few quiet moments, their breathing normalized and Peter stated, as well as questioned, "You still have your socks on."

Karen looked down and they both laughed. "It was a little cold in here."

"You want me to put the thermostat higher or something, babe?"

She turned to him with an all-encompassing sweep of her eyes that lovingly took in all his facial features. Peter recognized Karen's longing as she said, "Nah. I'm warm now." He kissed her forehead and went back to playing with her loose, curly hair as she reached over to take off the socks. She threw them across the bed where they landed on his pants, which, before the sex, had landed on his chair.

From his peripheral view, Peter could see Karen's gaze move from socks to pants, and then stay there as her head lay sideways on his chest. For a moment Peter thought that her focus on his jeans stemmed from his inadequate performance, but he dismissed that idea as soon as he thought it. Karen got more out of their sex then he did and told him so in a round about way months before.

She said that feeling him inside her was "like home." He wasn't sure what that meant, but from what he did know it was obvious that Karen hated her actual home and made every effort to avoid being there—sometimes even hiding in Peter's room so his parents wouldn't suspect an overnight guest. Though he only saw her father briefly when they were still freshmen at Buffalo, her mother lived in the city and he met her enough times to find her pleasant. On one occasion he asked Karen about her need to always be out. It was during one of her secret sleepovers. Instead of answering the question she said something vague about him not knowing everything and then pulled his pants down to avoid more talking. Lying back on his bed Peter noticed sobs that Karen tried to muffle but which he heard anyway.

It was with that same hunger for home that Karen slowly rubbed her hands over Peter's flat stomach, trying to avoid looking at his jeans. Peter knew, if only unconsciously, that having him around made Karen feel healed somehow. But as she rubbed his body, trying to stitch together hidden wounds, she just couldn't look away from his pants. Eventually she said, "Peter, some of your clothes are just so sloppy. You know, you don't always have to buy them two sizes bigger."

He chuckled. "That's just what I'm comfortable wearing. I like my skin to breath."

"I guess. Well, at least your pants don't hang off your ass. If they did I never would've talked to you."

"If that's what you say. But I remember you looking all in my face at Joanne's party."

She lifted her head off his chest to look at him with a slight smile and wide-open eyes. "Oh really? That's what you think?"

"Uh huh."

"I *was* looking at you. But I was thinking to myself 'why does this guy's T-shirt sleeve go past his elbow. Does he need help dressing himself?'"

"Whatever." His cheery look disappeared at the slight jab.

"Aww." She kissed him on the cheek. "You know you're sexy. Just…let's go shopping together next week or something."

"That's the second time I've heard you say that. Babe, I like to wear what I like to wear. It's my style and I don't need you trying to change me."

"I'm not trying to change you. I love you. But how you present yourself sometimes is a little…" She searched for the right word. "Rough?" not sure if she found what she was looking for.

Karen hopped out of bed and walked around to the closet, which was closer to Peter's side. She opened its door and said, "Baby, you live a few streets away from the Guggenheim. Your parents own half a block in Brooklyn. Your neighbors examine my skin when we leave the building together. You come from money, so, you know, you don't gotta look like you're living in a trap rap video."

Peter's calm, brought on by his orgasm, was being replaced by an uncomfortable tenseness. He looked at Karen as she stared into his closet with an expression of disappointment—the corners of her mouth were tight and stretched sideways.

"Like this shirt. It's straight out of a BET video."

"Now you sound silly. You're not black?"

"And half Seneca, but that doesn't mean I have to wear what the TV says brown people wear. And it's weird that you're white and you think that's what you should do." She slipped on one of his T-shirts. Its neckline reached the shoulders of her slight frame and hung off her body like she was a hanger. Her breasts created small curves in the otherwise straight drop the fabric made to her knees.

"I feel like I'm wearing a tent."

"Take my shirt off, Karen."

"I will. Just trying to show you how silly this stuff can look. Unless you're trying to be, like, some kind of street guy."

Peter slowly got off of the bed. He looked Karen in the eyes and said, "Cut it out. Take it off."

"I will." She turned to her left and looked at the mirror that hung from inside the closet door. Hunching her shoulders slightly, Karen made a scowl and said to herself, "Yo yo, son! I'm K-dog. I'll fuck that ass up if you try to pull that bullshit on me. I ain't the one. I ain't a punk."

Peter's face lost all expression as a patchwork of images from his past forced themselves together in his head. He remembered getting punched in the chest by his middle school bully over unintended insults; getting his watch—a gift from his father—stolen when coming home late from the movies; feeling shunned by peers for liking the wrong kind of clothing. Peter began to rage as he remembered times when he cried to himself about bruises and his inability to fight back when his manhood was questioned.

Still talking to the mirror Karen said, "I ain't soft." Again, in a move that was more reflex than anything else, Peter quickly pulled his arm back, made a fist as hard as he ever had, and landed it on the right side of Karen's face.

She was lifted off the ground, hit the wall a few feet away and collapsed on the floor. Not quite unconscious, she put her hand on her face in shock as her eyes shifted left to right—looking for a reason for the sudden attack. Peter could see her eyes stop moving as she came to her own conclusions about his reasons for striking her. She began to cry, and in a low, hushed voice said, "I was just joking. I'm sorry. I was just joking. I'm sorry Peter…" She repeated the words over and over again as Peter looked down at her. He was also in shock over what had just happened, but his face was still void of expression and his fists were still balled up tight as he felt a rush of emotions—a mixture of shame, strength, power, and repulsion.

Peter would apologize for hitting Karen. She would accept it. She would lie to people about what happened to her face. He would tell her that he loved her. She would need to believe it. She would believe it.

He would hit her again.

NO HIDING PLACE

His parents named him Edouard, or rather, that's what his mother named him. It was the first thing she said as the doctor wiped the blood and plasma from her baby's face and placed him in her weak arms. The rest of her body was equally weak, but she maintained enough energy to hear Edouard's first cry, and cry along with him and her husband as she kissed them both. Both mother in father ecstatic at seeing their first child and both trembled with the thought that together, out of love, they brought a life into the world that would shine brighter than they ever could, for long after their lights had blinked out. His mind unhindered by pain killers, Edouard's father was able to hold on to two thoughts. First he thought that he could never be happier than his was that day. Second, he was upset because he didn't at all like the name chosen for his son.

He wanted Federico, but slowly abandoned the argument

during the second trimester when the pain of pregnancy morphed into the look of pregnancy. His pitiable, semi-immobile wife, with her swollen body parts and needy ways, made him feel that it would be unseemly to argue with her. She ask, "Honey can you go to the store and get me some mangos?" He had just went to the store only an hour before with the salted fish that she asked for, but lying in bed with a face constantly wrinkled from mild to severe spasms he never argued. He looked at her with a smile and thought, "I will love you, and our child, for as long as I'm alive." Then he's walk out into the snow and curse repeatedly at the lazy super who hadn't deiced the front steps of the building. It was the same with the name. And so he accepted the name Edouard as he accepted the snowy midnight mango runs and the kiss from the mother of his child who lay on the birthing bed in the Kings County Hospital obstetrics unit.

She was grateful for the support, and as tired as she was, she reached for him and they both looked at their newborn son. They were entranced by his beautiful face and tried to divine some meaning from the lines on it. Without saying so to each other, they tried to guess at the future ahead of him, based on their own past.

Edouard's father, Francis, was born in La Saline, an area of Haiti where ditches were as common as streams of open sewage were as common as poorly built homes were as common as hungry children. That is to say, they were very common. Francis had seen five lifetimes worth of all four in his childhood alone as he trekked through his neighborhood chasing stray pets and rolling wooden wheels with sticks alongside friends. Francis grew up at a time when the country was run by its president-for-life, Jean-Claude "Baby Doc" Duvalier. Baby Doc's father, "Papa Doc," was also president-for-life and passed down the title to his son together with the wealth he accumulated from murder and large-scale grift.

The cross-generational kleptocracy robbed Francis of a well-funded school, decent healthcare, and food that reached above subsistence standards. Though his environment was filled with a constant instability, Francis was never conscious of how poor he was. He joked with classmates in his dilapidated, for-profit grade school. He memorized French verbs and basic math in his mother's ventilated shack of a house. When he got older, Francis later gained skills as a mechanic and dreamed of a job fixing cars when he graduated high school.

He would often tell his friends something like, "I won't be rich, but there will always be work. From what I see, that's the most important thing a job can offer." He was confident he would have at least that, or more, when the country's dictator fled in panic to live comfortably in France with the millions he had stolen from the miserable nation.

Francis was eighteen when Haitians ousted their ruler and elected their first president—a priest named Jean-Bertrand Aristide—who raised the minimum wage and pushed through other minor reforms. The effects of which were evident to Francis when he traveled through Port-Au-Prince on the weekends to drink with friends and fuck random women he met at zouk clubs.

"Hey, Francis!" He heard from his cousin Pierre one late Saturday night at *Labadee Manoir*. It's was the a week after the election and Francis was holding a beer as he smiled with a few other cheerful men and women that were doing the same. Pierre walked toward them holding his own beer and his own woman.

"What's up, cousin!" Francis replied as he leaned over and gave Pierre a tipsy hug "It's good to see you. Everyone's celebrating our new president and the absence of that motherfucker Duvalier! Here's to him and his bitch catching a bullet in the face." Francis raised his bottle and a few of his friends did the same. "It's a new day for Haiti."

One of the women said, "it's a new day for all of us. We can finally get this country on the right road."

As apolitical as he was, even Francis was able to enjoy the common understanding that the people who made life in his country so hard, were now gone. He smiled at Pierre, who knocked bottles with him before saying, "It's a new day, but how long will it last?"

"Now, why would you say something like that?"

Pierre waved his hand and said, "Eh, it's nothing."

"Don't ruin this for us!" Francis laughed, "But what are you thinking, cousin? Why the pessimism, eh?"

Pierre roughed up his younger cousin's hair, "Cause I read history books instead of keeping my head under car hoods. But who knows, maybe this will work out differently".

Pierre's girlfriend grabbed his beer and yelled, "Here's to different!"

They all cheered and the conversation shifted to old high school friends and possible travel plans outside of the city that most of them had never left.

Francis didn't care to keep up with local news, so as he danced, fucked, and worked under car hoods, he never felt the stirrings of a coup. He didn't know that, internationally, Haiti's new president was being described as an insane, narcissistic communist; he didn't know that all the western countries were calling for his removal.

What Francis did notice, and what made him flee the

country as quickly as possible, was a coalition of old Baby Doc cronies who had organized with former military henchmen under a new banner. With the help of the United States's National Endowment for Democracy, they began organizing paramilitary death squads that massacred anyone they felt was responsible for the first free election in the country's history. Francis was walking away from his last bit of fun at the local clubs when he saw one of these squads, armed with sugarcane machetes, bust into a bar and start chopping off heads and arms.

Among the butchered were some of Francis' high school friends who didn't pursue the same pleasures as he did. They mainly spent their weekends talking to other Haitians about social issues and organizing movements. For this, they had their brains blown out the side of their skulls, or had their vaginal walls torn by gang rapists who never bothered to use condoms as they spread disease and misery on a scale not seen since the country's first attempt at democracy earlier that same century.

In La Saline, Francis had seen the remains of his dead, and badly burned, cousin. Pierre was smarter, older, and wiser than Francis. Looking down at the lifeless and violated body of a man he had always looked up to forced Francis to his knees on that dark night. It was a mixture of mourning and awareness that shocked him beyond what his life of poverty had prepared him for. He became acutely aware that, though he lived a life devoid of politics, he was in real danger of being swept away in a terror that was less about politics than it was about power—exercising it and keeping it. With his mother dead the year before and no children that he was aware of, Francis found his way across the border to the Dominican Republic.

The kind of life he was leaving behind became obvious at the borderline. Haiti didn't have much in the way of environmental regulations, leaving both native and foreign corporations alike to abuse the land as much as they did the people. This had the effect of making the grass, literally, greener on the other side of the border.

With one foot on overworked dirt and the other on rich soil, Francis moved on. He kept moving until he found himself near San Juan de la Maguana.

He made a life for himself near the outskirts of the little city by fixing cars and performing other mechanical small jobs. Though he tried to continue his life as he had left it in Haiti—full of drudgery alongside superficial pleasures—he couldn't stop dreaming about the dead bodies he had seen. Francis's sleep was filled with recurring nightmares about the time he was approached by members of the rebellion.

Walking through a small town on his way east Francis had just left a dingy restaurant someone had set up in their shed of a home. He caught sight of a group of armed men and began to walk the other way when one hollered, "Hey you!"

With his back to them Francis froze. The same voice yelled out, "Are you deaf? Get the fuck over here!"

Francis crossed his eyes, turned around, and walked towards the men with an awkward gait, as if his right knee couldn't bend.

Approaching the one who called him Francis stuttered, "H-hello officer."

The man held a Ruger 10/20 with a banana clip longer than a toddler's arm. He looked at Francis with an expression of annoyance mixed with a soft hate as he said, "What's your name?"

"J-Jean-Robert officer."

"Are you from here?"

"Yes s-sir. I was walking home when you c-called. Am I d-doing anything wrong?"

"Maybe." The officer took a quick overall look at Francis, the hate in his face disappeared but the annoyance of a furrowed brow remained as he asked, "Do you know anyone in the neighborhood who's in Lavalas?"

"I don't. I don't know what…"

"The rebel group you idiot."

"I don't…"

"Hey, don't play dumb with me." Hate had returned to the man's eyes and he raised his gun with both hands to point it at Francis' forehead.

At that moment a humvee filled with United States contractors passed by. The mercenaries honked their horns and waved at the militia men.

The man holding the gun to Francis pulled his right hand off the trigger and waved back—the barrel still an inch away from skin. When he turned back to Francis, he looked on for a moment, let the Ruger drop down to his side and said, "Get the fuck out of here, retard." Without another word he walked to the now parked humvee. Francis made his way in the opposite direction, traumatized by being so close to his own death, but relieved that he didn't have to piss his pants in order to make himself appear even more wretched.

In the Dominican Republic, Francis had night sweats thinking of an alternate ending where large caliber rounds cut him into pieces, but he was somehow still alive to see everything that he loved burn up in a hell on earth.

In his little part of town Francis was known as a fixer, but not as a smiler. That changed the day he met Edouard's mother.

Edouard's mother, Estefani, was born and raised in the hilly areas around San Juan de la Maguana. She grew up poor, but not surrounded by the same fear that gripped Francis's family and friends. Her father and brother worked on their farm and grew the things they needed to live. For extra money, her mother worked in the city as a maid for a well-off couple who were five shades lighter than Estefani, her family, or Estefani's neighbors—many of whom had fled from Haiti generations before when another massacre, sponsored by another US president, lead to mass immigration.

That generation found themselves running into another dictator, Rafael Trujillo, who was trained by the American military, and followed the well-trodden path of other takers and killers. His favorite people to kill were Haitian immigrants and, in a vicious act of mass murder that Estefani's family somehow avoided, Trujillo ordered what Dominicans called "the cutting." The euphemism ended with government troops going into the hillsides and slaughtering thousands of people.

Estefani's oldest brother, Manuel, told her stories about it when she was a child.

Keeping her up late at night he would spin ghoulish tales about outlandish escapes from death.

"There were about thirty of them. Army men. All seven feet tall. Almost like giants. They had seen grandma in the town earlier and followed her trail up to the mountains like well-trained hunters."

"How could they follow her?" Estefani would ask, "Grandma is too smart to leave any clues."

"Of course grandma is smart. But no matter how smart you are a good hunter knows what to look for."

"Like... Like a wolf?"

"Exactly. These men were like wolves, but instead of sharp teeth they had machine guns as big as a baby cow." Estefani's eyes widened at the analogy so Manuel continued, "The guns had bullets as big as my thumb." He stuck his fat thumb in Estefani's face to illustrate. With a slight giggle she pushed it away. Manuel continued, "And each of these wolves had two of these guns."

"Did they find grandma?"

"They noticed her footprints in the mud leading into the graveyard at Santa Maria church so they followed. Grandma was hiding among the tombstones, but could hear the soldiers coming. Their mission was to find her and kill her, and she knew it.

"She couldn't be seen, but she had nowhere to hide in a graveyard. Then she figured it out. She looked for a grave that had just been dug. One where there wasn't too much dirt and the dirt that was there would be loose. She saw one and as the soldiers got closer, she started digging with her own two hands. Finally, the soldiers entered the graveyard looking for her. They saw nothing until one man spotted the open grave. He called another to him and pointed out the dirty casket. Like a wolf he could smell that grandma was near. And so he *jumped* into the hole and *pulled* open the casket..." Manuel paused, then widened his eyes to instill a bit of anticipation into the narrative. "But all they found was a fresh corpse. The smell was enough to make the soldier climb out of the grave. He and his partner continued their search, but would never find grandma."

"Where was she?" Estefani shouted.

"She was hiding where the soldiers would never look. She had jumped in the casket, but hid under the dead body that was there."

"Ewwww!"

"She lay there for days until it was safe to come out. Though the wolves were all around her, she found a way to stay safe. Many, many others were not as lucky." Getting up he said, "Okay little girl, it's time for you to go to sleep"

"I don't want to."

"And grandma didn't want to sleep next to a dead body. But we have to do what we have to do. And you have to go to sleep."

The bedtime stories thrilled, but mostly frightened Estefani as she closed her eyes and lay on the floor mat that was also her bed. Manuel, though, knew that there was a much more boring truth to The Cutting: anyone who was black was asked to say the Spanish word for parsley. If their tongues had been trained in Haitian Creole rather than Spanish they would have trouble pronouncing it and, summarily, they would be shot in the face and left to decompose on the lush, green Dominican grass that lay beyond the Haitian border.

Since she was a child, Estefani had soaked up stories like these and became a student of the history of brutality that shrouded her island like a thick blanket—creating an aggressive heat while also blocking out the sun. Remnants of Trujillo's administration still controlled much of the country after his death and Estefani found that out at a young age as well.

Her aunt, a breathtaking woman, was seen as a kind of prize that one of the local gangster-politicians believed was his to take. As a little girl brought along to a get-together, Estefani saw her aunt reject the small man in the middle of the medium-sized crowd. His nose flared and he spoke a few serious words before angrily walking away.

Later that night, when Estefani ran outside to chase a stray dog, she saw them both next to the brightly lit back doorway. Some more words were said and her aunt was slapped across the face, then thrown down onto the dirt where she was raped with a gun to her head. Estefani watched in silence and horror with her head peeking from behind the corner of the house. After a minute she slowly walked back to the house to quietly cry in front of adults who didn't ask any questions. A few weeks later her aunt disappeared. Estefani knew then, at the age of ten, that she had to leave that country.

At nineteen she had mapped out a plan: when to leave, how to leave, and where in the United States she could go. From what she knew about other nearby countries— Guatemala, Ecuador, El Salvador, Cuba, México, Puerto Rico, almost the entire South American continent—they had little more to offer than what she had.

Estefani worked in a free-trade zone as a seamstress sewing cartoon characters and swoosh logos onto shirts. The company was a third party vendor with a name that sounded like it was pulled from a thesaurus entry for the word "unassuming". That was exactly what the factories looked like from the outside. The series of large grey boxes held rows of sewing machine, sorting devices, and packing material that the mostly female staff used to create and ship shirts for Nike to the tune of \$.02 a minute—the unit of time Nike used to measure productivity.

Estefani sat in front of her sewing machine as those minutes went by. Needles moved in and out of fabric to patch together clothes that would sell for more than her entire week's paycheck.

Camilla, the woman who sat next to Estefani on the row of cheap seats, asked, "What plans do you have this weekend?"

"Rest. Maybe read a little. I don't think I have the energy for anything else."

"You sure?"

"Pretty sure. Why?"

"Well, I'm having a *chercha*. You know, some good music, maybe some cute guys..."

"I think I'll be fine with my book."

"Damn. You don't do much beside work do you?"

Estefani chuckled and said, "I do... sometimes. But pay now and play later. If I rest this Saturday I can work longer hours and the closer I'll be to leaving."

"The job."

"Yeah. That too."

"I'm not saying you've got to get drunk, or fuck a man on my kitchen floor..." Estefani laughed "just that I'm trying to get a little fun going. But if you don't wanna come that's fine"

"I'm glad you understand."

They continued to sew until Camila eventually said, "My brother asked me to invite you. He thinks you're beautiful."

"Are you done trying sell me? Beside your brother isn't that cute."

"Hey, he looks like me."

"Exactly. He's a man and shouldn't look like his younger sister."

After they both laughed Estefani asked, "What time do you want me there?"

Her planned to show up, talk for a few then leave. She knew that escaping the Caribbean was her only option if she was to avoid the same fate as her Aunt, or her brother who lost his right foot working a factory job outside the farm to gain extra money. Her plans were paramount, except for the night that she met Francis.

At Camila's house party Estefani leaned against a pastel green, chipped-paint wall drinking soda and chatting with a few other co-workers. She talked about music while inadvertently grabbing the attention of every man in the room who caught sight of her curvy body, beautiful face, and bright eyes. Francis was among those men, but memories of death had tamed him of his earlier desires. He admired her like a star in the sky that he had no thought of reaching for. He was too tired to aspire and contented himself with just quietly admiring.

Soon, however, he found himself dancing to a rhythm that forced him to his feet. The melody moved him to where he needed to close his eyes for a moment to appreciate it. When he opened them, he saw Estefani dancing alone next to him. He reached for her and they danced through the rest of that song as well as the next four. He held her hands tightly, but without his earlier, immature passions.

After their last song finished Francis said, "Thank you for the dance, my love. You made me feel very lucky." He bowed his head slightly with the same wide and warm smile he shined on her throughout their dance. She nodded in response. He walked to grab his hat and said goodbye to Camila's brother as well as the rest of the people he knew. Estefani watched him. He looked sincere; he looked kind; he looked good.

As he walked out of the house, down the hilly path to his own one room home, Estefani called out his name. He turned around and walked to her as she walked to him.

"You know," she said, "You're a really good dancer."

"Thank you. I spent huge chunks of my life doing only that. If I could impress you, then those years weren't in vain." He offered his hand to her. "I know you're Camila's friend, but I never got your name."

She grabbed his hand and said, "My name's Estefani."

"That's a beautiful name. Estafani, I don't know if you have any free time this week, but If you do, I would like to take you dancing, or to just get us something to eat, and get to know you better." He maintained his warm smile.

Not letting go of his hand she said, "I think that's the nicest date invite I've been given."

"I hope that's worth something."

"It's worth *one* date."

She held onto his hand for a few more moments in the same way she would during their first night out. It was the same way she held him when they first made love. Their fingers interlocked and he would hold her just a tightly while softly kissing her cheek and lips. He would hold her hand as they got married. They felt safe as they held each other and moved to the United States where they only let go so they could hold their child, Edouard.

The two saw their lives in the shifting shape of their baby's familiar face. Through the lens of their own history, they could also see the path that the life of their baby boy would take.

Edouard would grow up in a loving home where his father would teach him to love other people, and his mother would teach him to love himself. He would try his best in the Crown Heights Brooklyn neighborhood to actively step over the trappings of poverty. The everyday scenes inspired by drugs, greed, and deprivation would all capture his attention as his peers indulged in all the damaging things that felt good at the moment.

His middle school would have a glut of students, while at the same time be starved of all the things needed to teach them—the things needed to divert Edouard's mind from the violence around him that was both literal and figurative.

While helping him the night before a test his mother would hold his history book and quiz him, "What are the main principles of Wilsonian Idealism as reflected in his fourteen points?"

At age eleven Edouard would look down on their kitchen table, searching for an answer in the patterns of the faux marble top. "Um… Um.. Emphasis on self-determination of peoples." Estafani would lift her index finger. "Advocacy of the spread of democracy." Middle finger. "Advocacy of the end of communism." Ring finger. "Opposition to isolationism and non-interventionism." Pinky finger. "And… and" Looking down at the pattern for answers he finally said, "In favor of intervention"

With her thumb up, Estafani gave her son a high five. They both smiled and she said, "I think you're going to do very well tomorrow."

"Yeah, I'm gonna ace that test." Walking to the fridge Edouard poured himself some water and said, "Can I ask a question, mommy?"

"Anything."

"Did you ever need to learn this stuff when you were in school? I mean, I know that DR has different kinds of schools, but did you or poppy have to take tests like this. About stuff like this?"

"Like this, yes. Although poppy might have a different story, I went to nice schools and we learned a lot."

"Yeah, I guess. I just… Have you ever had to use anything from those tests in real life. Like when you left school."

"Of course not. This is just to pass a test."

"But why?" He would sit back down and begin drinking.

"So you can get to a higher grade. And then get a degree. And then get a good job."

"Okay. But some of this stuff is so boring. When I become an architect do I have to know about Woodrow Wilson?"

"I'm not an architect. I don't know. I would not think so though. Listen, you learn this information so that your life will be better than mine or poppy's. You are the reason we work so hard. We put everything we have into you so that you will be better than either of us. Passing these tests is a part of that. Now, there *is* a benefit to knowing things that you may never use as an architect. Things that will make your decisions smarter and will keep your mind strong. Go get me your laptop."

Edouard would run to his room, rummage around drawings of gravity defying spires and dirty clothes until he returned with his laptop. Estafani would call him to her side with an "Aqui" and he would watch her surf the net until she fell upon a book titled, "Gunboat Diplomacy in the Wilson Era."

"Now this is a book that is *not* boring. I don't think it will help you become an architect, but I do think that it will make your mind stronger. It will help make your decisions smarter. I can get it for you if you want."

"What's it about?"

"It's a history book."

"Another history book?" He laughed "I already have two from school, mommy."

"No you don't."

He wouldn't understand his mother's confusing message, but the mystery of something undiscovered would move him enough to respond, "If you get it, can we read it together?"

"Yeah. And if you like it we can get more books, interesting books, on other subjects."

"If I don't want to, can I say no."

"Anytime. But you will have to know the books your schools give you. Now let's get started on English homework."

"If we have to."

"We have to. Now gimme a kiss before you get that book."

Edouard would continue to read with his mother while also keeping a safe distance from the kind of life that led to no life. He would maintain a relatively high GPA along with his independent reading list; his father would take him camping or on out-of-state road trips when he wasn't working at the local mechanic shop; his mother would teach him how to cook proper mangú and arroz con gandules while talking to him about big ideas and the dreams he hoped to fulfill one day. Edouard would also stay out late with friends and occasionally smoke weed while trying to get his dick sucked by local girls. He'd keep up this healthy balance until he turned fifteen.

At that age his neighborhood would see police presence increase dramatically. A new precinct would be set up near their apartment building with the results being a slight decrease in crime and a drastic increase in the amount of Edouard's (now Eddie's) friends who would be thrown in jail or snatched up on charges like resisting arrest when asking why they were being told to empty their pockets.

After a few months, Eddie, as well as his parents, would see other changes in their neighborhood. Construction on old vacant lots would reveal beautifully modern glass and steel apartment buildings. The people moving in would have more money than the long-time locals and this would be evident to Eddie for a few reasons. For one, most of them would be white, which, while Eddie would try to consciously fight the idea, had long ago become a sign of wealth and power to him. They'd also dress differently and carry themselves differently—in a way that would make Eddie uncomfortable for reasons he couldn't put a finger on.

Eddie would try to articulate his feelings to Francis on one of their trips to the Brooklyn museum.

Looking at art from Jean Dubuffet Eddie said, "She was coming from one of the new grocery stores—the one where Jenny's hair salon used to be. She looked at us strange. Like we were doing something out of place. Pascal called her a racist... I mean, he said she was racist. But I don't think so. I didn't get a feeling of fear or anger, just that something was off for her. Like we didn't make sense. It made me weird walking down the street *right on my block*."

"Things are really changing around here. It's not all black and white though." Francis would be silent for a few moment to gather his thoughts, and the vocabulary necessary to express it in the fourth language he was forced to learn. "I think it's a good idea for you to see people from different backgrounds. Almost everyone here is Haitian, so you've missed seeing things from another side." He would stop again and look at the painting while he talked. "Like you, that woman may have never seen too many black people in her life, other than on TV. Pascal may be right, but if she was racist, it was just out of ignorance."

"But doesn't it bother you that all these expensive, nice things are popping up, and they weren't here when it was just us. And even now that's it's here, we can't really afford it? I tried to get some potato chips at the new store and the cheapest one was a dollar!"

Francis would laugh and hearing how silly he sounded, so would Eddie, "That is quite a serious problem. I was talking to your mother about that just yesterday. The high price of junk food is gonna bankrupt us."

"I'm serious though dad."

"I know." Putting his hand on the boy's shoulder he would say, "These new people are making things hard for us, but most of them aren't to blame. They come here because they can not afford anywhere else. They are like leaves blowing on winds that they have little control over. We'll figure things out, but if you want to be mad, be mad at the wind that brought them here. I can tell you, I've seen some... horrific things growing up. I survived them and I'm stronger, I think. This is nowhere near that bad. We'll survive it and hopefully be stronger."

"Dad, you never talk about what happened when you were young in Haiti."

"What do you mean? I tell you all the time. I had a great childhood in a poor country. Then I had to leave when the coup happened."

"You never talk about that. The coup."

"It was everything you and your mom read about in your books. There's nothing more I can add other than that I'm glad you're here. I'm glad me and your mother are here. I'm glad we're all finally safe."

"I understand."

Francis would look Eddie in the eyes for a few seconds with a smile. "Good. Now let's move along. This Dubuffet stuff isn't as exciting as the website made it seem."

As the months ran on the changes would continue and soon Francis and Estafani's landlord would raise the rent well beyond what it had been. Their new rent, along with the stores and shops that now catered to the new residents, would increase their cost of living and drive them from their home of the previous seventeen years.

Their new neighborhood, further south in Brownsville, would be much rougher than their previous. It would take longer for Eddie's parents to get to work and it would be much harder to get the foods that they were used to buying. It would also become harder for Eddie to continue the balancing act he had cultivated for most of his life. Though he had already been accepted to a reputable college, his last year in high school would see his grades slip. He would spend more time in the streets trying to do more than just getting his dick sucked.

Francis and Estefani would worry about him a little, but would tell each other that he was just being young and that he would straighten up again once he left for college, a place far away from the negativity that surrounded them. Eddie would be on their minds as he sat on a park bench with four friends, laughing at a joke made about his history teacher's ill-fitting hairpiece. In the middle of the laughter, a squad car would pull up and the exiting policemen would ask what was going on. What were the five boys doing out there? Eddie and his friends would stare back silently, not trying to hide the disdain in their eyes for being asked, essentially, why did they exist.

One of the officers would ask, "You little shits don't have

anything to say?"

Again, silence, until one of the boys would begin to walk away. With a sudden movement, the officers would walk quickly toward the group. Their hands on their holstered guns, one of them would shout, "Don't move! Stay right there!" At this the boy would turn his walk into a run for the nearby housing project courtyard. The officer closest to him would give chase and leave the other cop to remain, his gun now drawn on the four remaining teens. He shouted again, "Don't move!"

"What did we do wrong?" is what Eddie would try to say, but after "what" the nervous policeman's gun would go off and shoot Eddie in the chest. The fatal shot would lead to a publicized funeral and, later, a failure to indict the murderer. Leaving the courthouse, reporters would ask Francis if he intended to sue the city. Both Estefani and Francis, almost choking on their own tears, would confirm that they planned to sue.

Their civil suit would drag on for two devastating years wherein they had to regularly relive the very thing they moved to America to escape. They would lose the case and afterwards try to return to something of a normal life, minus the only child they had. Every so often Francis would watch the news and hear of stories similar to Eddie's. The parents would look like him or Estefani, and the child always looked like their son.

The country where Francis was born was a place he could never go back to because of the turmoil that would meet him if he returned. Because of new laws, their dark skin and Haitian ancestry would deny him and Estefani the ability to go back to the country where she was born. Listening to the news, both nations would seem eerily similar to where they now lived. Francis and Estefani would miss their son with a pain that made every breath hurt. Every so often they would succumb to that pain and cry on each other's shoulders as they realized that they had *never* been safe. That there was nowhere they could they be free.

They both caught a glimpse of this life as they looked at Edouard's miniature face, still wet from his trip though the birth canal and into the light of the world. Not mentioning anything to the other, they simply sighed and kissed as they wondered about the place they had brought this new life into—a place that was supposed to be his home.

ANGELS

THE NEWBORN LOOKED LIKE a mutant raisin. That was all Kathy could think of as she stared her niece in the face. The pale thing lay on her sister-in-law's chest and looked back with pupils like black dots that couldn't see more than a foot away. She was wrinkled, with facial features that Kathy couldn't describe other than to say that they were there. Her nose was there; her ears were there; her mouth was there. They were all there, but they were as shapeless as a dream. The only thing Kathy could say for certain was that the wrinkles in the baby's skin made her look like a raisin that had been exposed to some transmogrifying chemical out of a comic book.

After a few seconds of eye contact, the baby began to slowly move its mouth, working herself up to a cry that made Kathy stand up straight when the sound eventually came out. As she set her pocketbook down on a chair next to her mother, Kathy asked, "So what are you going to name her?" Hospital policy only allowed two guests during visiting hours, but Jacob managed to sneak in his parents, his sister Kathy, and some in-laws that Kathy didn't know by name.

Jacob said, "We decided that if it was a boy, I would name it. But if it was a girl Tanya would."

Jacob then looked at Tanya lying on the hospital bed. With the attention of the room on her, she held her newborn daughter and said, "Angela." Tanya's slight eyes were dull, her skin glittered with beads of sweat, and her black hair was tossed across the pillow with no care at all. She seemed happy nonetheless. She looked warmly at the infant girl in her hands—lifting the child off her chest to look at her face. "She's our little angel."

"And what would you two have named it if it were a boy?" Kathy asked.

This time Tanya looked at Jacob who smirked and said, "Jacob Rajeshwer Junior."

Everyone in the room, except for Tanya's parents, laughed at his lack of imagination. "Hey, it's got roots plus Jacob's a good Christian name."

Kathy said, "I forgot that's a thing with you now."

"No need to mock my beliefs 'cause you're jealous of my cool name."

"No one's mocking, Jacob." Kathy kissed him on the cheek and said hello to the unknown in-laws who were orbiting Tanya and Angela. They all exchanged quick, friendly smiles that only took a second or so away from their joyful and quiet observation of the baby. Kathy took off her jacket and got ready to take up space for at least the next hour. As soon as she sat down, though, she remembered the present she had left in the car.

"I'll be right back," she told Jacob. "I forgot something in my car."

Almost no one took notice as Kathy got up and walked into the hallway, but Jacob followed behind her—late by a few seconds and behind her by only a dozen feet.

"I'll go with you. I need a cigarette break or something. Maybe we can catch up."

"I don't smoke, but yeah, I'll stand outside with you."

"That's what I said. I need a cigarette break." He laughed. "I'm the one looking at dirty diapers and sleepless nights. Be grateful you don't have any stresses to smoke away."

"I guess," she said as he caught up to her. They walked to the elevator, and she let out a sigh that Jacob didn't notice. Kathy hadn't talked to Jacob in months. She hadn't seen him in almost a year. Her excuse, whether legitimate or not, was that she had just been promoted. Her career wasn't necessarily more important than her brother, but she enjoyed it, and there was only so much she could do with an ocean between them. Really, they lived in other worlds. What could she do about that? Nothing was the answer.

The news about her niece's birth was extraordinary, but also annoying. As the new head of marketing, she had broken through the glass ceiling, which in India could be more appropriately described as the Kevlar barrier. Those years working harder and longer than anyone else was the ammo she used to break through and get that executive office, and a title that let people know that she mattered. All of it might be in jeopardy if she decided to rush out because of personal issues. She had deadlines coming up and print ads to give the final okay on. Leaving might have meant that she wasn't capable of handling the responsibility.

All of this weighed heavy on Kathy's mind along with even deeper concerns that made her sigh again as she and Jacob exited the elevator into the hospital lobby.

After getting her gift of baby pajamas from the backseat of a rented car, Kathy stood beside the revolving front door of the hospital next to Jacob who had already begun smoking.

"Missed you at Dad's birthday," Jacob said.

"Same here. There's only so much I could do about a sick pilot though."

"Not blaming you. Just saying you were missed."

"Thanks."

"Hey, thinking of sticking around for a few? There's a great tandoori spot five minutes away. We can get dinner for everyone. Or a Columbian spot. Or a Greek spot."

Kathy rubbed Jacob's slightly rounded stomach and said with a laugh, "Or Pakistani or Chinese. I'm sure you've been to every one of them a few times, huh?"

"I've been eating for two!" Jacob laughed along with Kathy and said, "One of the perks of the new neighborhood. If you stay for a few days, I could show you some of the little multicultural miracles of Jackson Heights."

Kathy looked away with a sad smile that said that she wanted to avoid conflict. Jacob disappointment was imperceptible, except for the slight drop in his eyes as he looked closer at the puddled ground.

"I'm just glad you could make it for this. It may not look like it 'cause I'm so damn suave, but I'm really overwhelmed here. Her parents like me, but they're pretty old school and still not over the fact that, besides loving dim sum, I'm not even close to being Chinese. They can make things uncomfortable sometimes. Now we have a baby, and they're already talking about how they're going to do this, and how we've got to do that." Jacob shook his head, and Kathy gave a supportive pat on the back in an attempt to reconnect in some meaningful way. He continued, "Then that gets me thinking about the fact that I really am a father now. I keep thinking about what's going to happen in the next few years. What about when she's in high school? I've got, like, these psychic powers now and I can see ahead to puberty, boys, paying for college—which should be like a billion dollars a semester by the time she's able to go. Kat, I'm really swimming right now. There's no solid ground under my feet." Jacob turned his head to look at Kathy, who was staring ahead contemplatively. The stormy wind was blowing back her curly brown hair. "You listening over there?"

"Yeah. Just a little distracted."

"About what? I just had a baby." Jacob took a pull from his cigarette. "Was hoping for an open ear."

"I'm sorry, Raj. Go ahead."

"It's Jacob, and don't worry about it."

Kathy pursed her lips. Jacob took his last pull from the dying cigarette.

"You know, I haven't seen you in months. You live, like, a twelve-hour flight away, and now that you've stopped by for a few hours to see your new niece, but you can't even talk?" Jacob dropped the cigarette and stepped on it as he said, "If you're going to be here, then be here. If not then you can head back to India. Tell Mumbai I said take a shower."

He was walking to the revolving door when Kathy said, "I'm pregnant." Jacob stopped moving for a moment, and then returned to where he had been standing.

He pulled out another cigarette and asked, "You have a boyfriend or a husband I don't know about?"

"No, I don't."

"Okay. First question. Are you sure? When you were in college, I remember you telling me what the doctor…"

"I remember," she interrupted Jacob. "Hormones, synchronization, etcetera. I wasn't supposed to be able to have a baby, but here it is. I'm pregnant, and I don't know what the hell to do."

"What do you mean you don't know what to do?"

"I mean just what I said. I don't know if I'm going to keep it or not."

From her peripheral view, Kathy could see his face wrinkle up. She expected no less. Despite the exoticness of Jacob and Tanya's ethnic differences, their life was right in line with the campiest family comedies of the 1980's. They met as juniors at Columbia College, they fell in love, he converted to her religion, they got a house in the second dullest of the five boroughs, and now they had a kid. In her eyes, *Jacob* was still a kid—the toddler, ten years her junior, who dug around in her makeup drawer and powdered his balls with her foundation. He was a little spoiled and easily shaken by things outside the norm.

"I don't really think you have a choice if you're pregnant." He looked at her with a mild mix of rapprochement and surprise. "You're having a baby, right?"

"Jacob, I didn't tell you so you could try and convert me. I don't want to hear what your man in the sky has to say about me being pregnant!"

"Look, I'm just saying…" Jacob stopped. He took another pull from his cigarette and said, "You're right. You know what? Let's take a quick ride to that Pakistani or Chinese place."

"I'm not hungry, Jacob."

"Obviously. I'm suggesting the ride as an excuse for us to talk. I want to know what the hell's happening with my sister."

"Okay. Only if you're buying, though."

"Goodness. How much do you make a year again?"

They walked into the light drizzle towards Jacob's car. After hitting the local streets, Jacob asked, "So, do you know who the father is?"

"Of course I do."

"Well, I'm just asking, Kat. These things happen I guess, and honestly, I don't know you that well anymore. I have no idea what my corporate sister is doing with her life, except dressing in *really* nice pants suits. I'm trying to find out what's going on."

"I guess you're right. There hasn't been much back and forth between us for a while."

"No, there hasn't been. But we can start. Tell me what happened."

Kathy looked out of the passenger side window as tiny droplets of rain collected on the glass. They grew bigger and bigger as they amassed more water until, eventually, they were blown away by the wind of the car's forward movement. She watched the cycle a few times, finding herself calmed by it. The muscles in her face relaxed, and she said, "About two months ago I was in a marketing conference. There was a pretty good presentation on how to approach social media." Her voice began to speed up as she talked. "The thing is that people say you need quality content but they don't understand what 'quality' means for different networks. What's good for Twitter won't necessarily work on Facebook. You have to be acutely aware of the what each…"

Jacob slowed the car down so he could safely stare at Kathy. He contorted his face—complete with raised eyebrows and curled lips—to express a dismissiveness that Kathy responded to with a smile.

"Got it. So, I had questions that I wanted to ask one of speakers on that panel. I caught up to him afterward, and we talked for about twenty minutes. He asked if I wanted to have drinks that night with him and some of his colleagues. We met. He was smart and gentlemanly and funny, and we went back to my hotel room."

"Ah."

"Yeah."

Jacob parked the car. "Let's get off here."

"This place isn't Pakistani or Columbian."

"No, but it's Thirty-seventh Avenue. There are plenty of food stands not scared of a little rain. Enough that we can get our bellies filled before we hit two blocks."

"Okay. You're still paying though."

"They're cheap, so we're good."

For Kathy, the light rain felt good. She didn't try to protect her face as she slowly walked to the Tibetan food cart on the corner. Jacob walked a little faster and ordered some dumplings while standing under the cheap plastic sheet that hung over the stand—meant to keep the cook, along with a single customer, dry. When Kathy got there, Jacob moved to offer her the coverage. She told him the rain wasn't bad enough for her to have to huddle in such a tight space. He jumped back in, and they waited for their food.

The avenue was busy with shoppers, and Kathy wondered if the reason Jacob stopped there was to have her watch the families going from store to store—adorable kids of all ages and backgrounds dragged their parents around to toy stores and restaurants.

Their order was for one, but Jacob got two forks and they ate as they walked on, leaving the car behind. With half-eaten meat in his mouth, Jacob said, "From what you've said it doesn't sound like a bad situation. If you know the father and he seemed like a nice guy, maybe it can work out if you go through with it."

"He doesn't even know."

"You haven't told the man you're pregnant?"

"No, I haven't. Jacob, are you telling me you've never had a one-night stand?"

"Don't tell Tanya, but yeah, once."

"Did you love her? Did you want to have children with her?"

"That's not the point…"

"Yeah, it is. What if you got one of those girls pregnant? Whether she told you or not doesn't change the fact that it would be hers and it would be in her body, and it would be up to her to decide what happens next. If you wanted it and she didn't, she wouldn't keep it. If you didn't want it and she did, she would keep it anyway."

"And if you do decide to keep it?"

"Then I'll tell him. Not until then though. I don't need someone in my car telling me what they think when they're not me."

"I think I can understand."

The rain got a little heavier, and they ducked under the awning of a local knick-knack store waiting for it to calm down.

"Does anyone else know about this?"

"Besides my doctor? No."

"Makes me feel pretty special, but why? Is there a specific

reason you wouldn't want to tell a friend or something?"

"Only that I don't want anyone to feel obliged to tell me what they think is best."

"Is that why you went to India in the first place?"

Kathy waited until she finished her last dumpling to ask, "What do you mean by that?"

"I mean you weren't raised over there. We both went to school a couple miles from here. You watched Voltron growing up. I watched Power Rangers. When I think about why you would want to go live in India, the only thing that comes to mind is that you just didn't want anyone around you anymore. Anyone you knew anyway. You didn't want the opinions of your family."

Kathy didn't reply, and they stood under the awning for a few minutes without a word between them. Jacob picked between his incisors with a toothpick from the Tibetan place. Soon the rain died down to a light drizzle again.

Kathy said, "Let's hit up that Mexican stand."

They walked in silence. When the two reached the truck, Kathy asked for "two pollo tostadas, please." The short order cook nodded, and Kathy stepped aside from the window to keep the growing line moving.

She said, "There's something to what you said. I love you, and Mom and Dad, but it's just that..." She shook her head in small movements that were meant more to communicate something to herself than to Jacob.

"It's just that I don't like knowing that there's some mold that people have for me. Even if it's well-intentioned, I don't want to feel obliged to anyone. That's what this pregnancy is about too. I love my job. I mean I genuinely enjoy it. I like going to work, and I like being the one who makes things happen. If I have a kid, all of that's over. My life will be over."

"Don't sound so dramatic, Kathy. You'd just have to adjust."

"How I live now, I can't adjust. That life will be over."

"You might be surprised how much better you're new might be, Kat. Look at this place. There's like six different countries represented on this taco line right now. From all over the world people are making babies. Some of them shouldn't, but no matter the place there's something wonderful and universal about holding a child in your arms. Your whole view on things change, and you might find yourself looking forward to adjusting your life for the life you've created. Look, I don't want to beat you over the head with my opinion of things, but if you're thinking about the trouble that comes with a kid…"

"Two pollo tostadas." The cook said.

Kathy and Jacob grabbed one each and stood on the side of the curb to eat. Jacob said, "Damn, this is gooood."

"Yeah, this guy's pretty all right."

After a few mouthfuls, Jacob said, "I wanted to say that you have help. No one's trying to put you in a box. You're a grown up and we all respect you, but we can have opinions, right? I'm not trying to tell you what you should do or who to worship." Kathy rolled her eyes. "But you might be missing out on a lot. And your one chance to have it." He let out a small burp before continuing. "If you do decide that it's a good idea, you'll have help. There are a lot of things that you can do when you have support. I'm sure you could afford to hire a nanny or something. Me and Tanya or Mom and Dad can take the kid for the summer. You know how many people in the family would stand the twenty hours of travel time just to see a baby."

"Yeah, but then what would be the point of me? I wouldn't be its mother, just the landlord, and I don't want that either."

Jacob replied, "Yeah, I know." The rain had stopped entirely as Kathy finished her last two sloppy mouthfuls of chicken and corn tortilla. The sky still held the promise of more, but as they stood there, things were still. A mother and her toddler had left one of the nearby clothing stores and walked towards the food truck. As they passed Kathy and Jacob, the little boy grabbed onto Jacob's long wool coat and tugged as he giggled. The mother pulled his hand loose and apologized before getting in line.

Jacob looked at where the child had touched him and saw that a shiny, sticky handprint—possibly from syrup—was left on the spot. Kathy laughed as she pointed at the five-finger mark that was no bigger than a playing card.

"He was cute though, Kat."

"Yes, he was. But that stain on your jacket? That's arguable. C'mon, let's get some samosas for Mom and Dad and head back to see your daughter."

"Okay. But let's get some souvlaki first."

After walking back to Jacob's car, they drove while Jacob pointed out small changes in the neighborhood that he noticed since moving in. New luxury condos and apartments were being built, and he lamented the slow disappearance of the community feel that he and Tanya moved there for. Kathy asked if they had planned to be there permanently, and he said that they made several plans, but they both knew that if change comes, they will welcome it.

They arrived at the hospital and walked through the revolving door into the cool, chemically tinged hospital air. As they entered the room, Tanya asked, "Where were you guys? We were getting a little worried."

"We just went to get my parents some samosas, baby." Looking at his in-laws he said, "Got you guys some dim sum too." They smiled kindly, but quietly, and looked back to their daughter and granddaughter. Jacob looked at Kathy and threw his hands up in silence. She smiled and walked passed him. Kathy joined them as they stared at her niece.

She stuck out her finger for Angela to grab and the newborn weakly held it for a few seconds while everyone oohed and aahed. Kathy oohed a little as well, but looking closer her smile disappeared as she began to see some defining features on the baby's face. She made a mental catalog of anything distinct. Angela had little ears that stuck out more than usual. Her nose was wide but not long. Not flat necessarily, but small. Kathy smiled again. Although she wasn't sure what her life was going to look like in the next few months, she knew for sure that her new niece was adorable.

STANDBY

A too-distant-to-be-heard smartphone alarm, a major car accident on the Yingbin Expressway, and a slow, eighty-something-year-old cab driver all conspired against me this morning. It's impossible for me to know what secret communications were had between my mobile device and the Chinese skeleton dressed in liver-spotted skin, but together they made me miss my flight by forty minutes.

My time in the taxi was filled with randomly blurted curse words and then, finally, acceptance as we eventually stopped at the Shanghai airport. I tried to take comfort in the fact that I hadn't arrived even close to my departure time. It would've twisted the knife in my back had I went running to the gate just to see the damn plane taking off—loosening gravity's hold on it while leaving me on the ground to shake my head in frustration.

Instead, what I got was a courteous, "Sorry, sir, but you

have missed your flight." The pretty clerk spoke almost perfect English, though she failed to master the art of contractions. With a smile as fake as plastic, she continued, "The next several flights to Los Angeles are all full as well. If you would like, I could place you on standby. When a seat becomes available, we can contact you."

She went on, and I listened intently while imagining my tongue between her thighs. The loneliness that plagues the divorced and stranded was driving me to obscene daydreams, though my expression remained the same as it had been when I walked through check-in. I sighed as my thoughts switched from the last time I actually held a woman to the depressing possibility of sleeping in an airport, waiting for some other idiot to miss their flight.

I agreed to standby and gave her my cell number to call when something opened up. Until then, I decided to walk around the airport and waste time.

My first stop was the duty-free store. While browsing for nothing in particular, I thought about what I should tell my supervisor. What excuse could I give for missing this coming Monday's sales meeting? I squeezed one of ten Norwegian stress dolls on the wooden plank shelf. Thinking that the reality of the situation might reflect poorly on me, I decided to omit the alarm clock from my story and send an email as soon as I felt like doing so—giving him something to read with his boiled eggs and black coffee breakfast. I'd write: Yes, everything went well. Yes, they liked the software. Yes, they want it set up in their headquarters here and their offices in the UK. The news would most likely excite him beyond what the pretty clerk could do for me.

Aside from liquor, the shop had nothing I was even remotely interested in buying—the stress doll's wholesome smile bulged grotesquely with each compression, and I put it away. With the slow-footed pace of a bum, I left to find some lunch.

The food court consisted of a few US franchises, but it was dominated by small, national chains that sold food I imagine McDonald's would make if its mascot were a drunk Chinese cook rather than a clown who loved kids. The smells from most of the chains were enough to keep me away. My month in China had had its moments, but it wasn't enough time for me to adjust to eating bite-sized pieces of food with flavors that didn't match. I was tired of pickled and fresh, hot and cold, sweet and sour.

After twenty minutes of aimless meandering, I passed by a small box of a restaurant selling salted fish. I stopped when a stray aroma drifting out from its serving area drew me back, without warning, to another time. Though the scent quickly morphed into something fairly unpleasant, my mind stayed in my grandfather's kitchen, watching him cook baccalà alla Livornese. My grandpa taught me what little I know about cooking, and as I stood there in the midst of strong fishy smells I tried to remember what he looked like when I was a kid; I tried to remember what he looked like the last time I visited him. I thought about it a little more, but those parts of my life were lost to me.

With the weight of my carry-on luggage holding me down in the crowded dining area, I shook my head in disappointment. The years of business trips that seemed to begin the day I took my first breath were all taking their toll on me. I was losing strength by the second and decided to let the smells weaving their way between the polite chatter push and pull me to my next stop. I hit stir-fried liver and onions and made a left. I walked past some "beggar's chicken" and slowed a bit before speeding up again at the first whiff of stuffed snake.

Walking in jagged zigzags, I kept moving as I tried to remember more than just the broad outlines of my grandpa's smile. Neither it or the finer details of my life outside of work were coming into focus. What that truly represented kept me weak and drifting until I almost walked into a sign that advertised the "All-American Restaurant." The logo was the name in Times New Roman with each word colored red, white, and blue respectively. Their picture menu distilled the American cuisine down to burgers and fries, but I also saw pizza and spaghetti that didn't look half bad. Not necessarily "All American," but I certainly didn't mind the error and decided to give the spaghetti a try while waiting for a plane to take me back home—however temporary that stay back home would be.

I ordered a plate, sat down, and looked at my phone. Would anybody call me besides the pretty clerk? Maybe my supervisor would wake up in the middle of the night and decide that he needed to hear my reassuring voice. Did he count? I told myself that he did and waited for my pasta.

It came, surprisingly, in a proper pasta bowl with a fork and spoon. I noticed small chunks of garlic and green peppers. They had been cooked perfectly, but the fact that they were fresh in the first place was enough to impress. I took another look around to reassure myself that indeed this was a small franchise restaurant with chairs made of fiberglass painted to look like wood.

I twirled the fork in the pasta and let the aroma waft into my busy nose. With my eyes closed and mouth opened, I remembered what was lost.

My grandpa's knees no longer allowed him to stand in his

kitchen for the long stretches of time needed to cook as well as he did, so I, along with my childhood friend turned-wife-for-six-months, ran around doing the prep work. The Queens Village kitchen was cramped. Like much of the old house, it was the same as it had been since I was two years old. The large windowsill above the sink was still cluttered with ceramic knick-knacks that reflected the hoarder mentality of a sweet old man who'd been through the Great Depression.

We chopped veggies, cleaned chicken, and handled everything that didn't require decades of experience and know-how. Grandpa came in every so often with kind words about what we were doing wrong. He eventually kicked us out and cooked what we had left as we waited in the living room.

Sherry and I were in the middle of our six months of marital bliss and looked on, unaware that we wanted totally different things out of life: I wanted children, and she wanted another woman. Her hair was still long then, and she pinched my arm playfully whenever I asked my grandfather if he was done yet. We both happily watched him as we sat on the living room floor out a childhood habit of not wanting to ruin the cheesy, Victorian-style furniture my grandfather had kept since my grandmother died.

He made spaghetti Caprese. Each piece of food he chopped, diced, or whatever came together like gold in an alchemist's lab, and he brought it into the living room with a smile. When I grabbed the plate, he gave me a kiss on the cheek.

In my grandfather's house, I had a home. Holding the hand of my soon-to-be ex-wife, I was a twenty-five-year-old child with facial hair and a job I tolerated. A year after our easy-going but heartbreaking divorce, I left New York, and work tried its best to fill in the holes in my world.

I missed having someone who cared about me. I missed my grandfather's cheek kisses, and I missed Grandpa's last days before his big heart eventually decided that it had done enough and needed to rest. His funeral was about five years ago, and it was one of only four times in which I had seen anyone in my family since leaving New York.

I finished the food and ordered a burger to eat later on the plane, or while waiting for one. Walking back to my gate, I sent an email to my supervisor so he would receive the good news when he woke up. In New York, though, it was midnight, and I figured that was still early enough to call.

I heard a cough on the other end, then a congested, "Hello."

"Hey, Kim. Is Sherry there?"

"Who is this?"

"Kim, it's Michael."

"Mike? Jesus, you know what time…"

"I know, I'm sorry. But is Sherry there?"

"Yeah, yeah. Gimme a second." I listened to mumbling in the background and smiled when I heard my friend and ex-lover cursing.

"Mike, you all right?" I smiled a little more as I heard the rarely asked question.

"Yeah, I'm doing good. In China right now."

"Haven't heard from you in I don't know how long. You sure everything is all right?"

"Just realized that I haven't heard a friendly voice in I don't know how long. Been too long I guess. Got time so I figured I should call some folks, starting with you. How are you doing?"

She chuckled and told me how she and Kim were doing. We settled on a weekend for me to visit New York for the welcome party she was going to have for me—she promised she'd invite women who were my type. In a series of jokes, I told her about the strange restaurant with the cheap chairs. We talked about visiting Grandpa's old place in Queens, and I cried for three minutes straight. It felt good.

I let her know about the clerk and that I didn't like how isolated and sad I'd been feeling lately. She was silent for a few seconds, seemingly caught off guard, but when she spoke again, she told me that it was all right. She understood, and she was there to listen.

DESPERATE LIVES

KEITH DIDN'T RECOGNIZE THE PEOPLE in the newspapers. The black-and-white pages were full of unfamiliar faces that belonged to people he would never meet—known for doing extraordinary things outside of the world he lived in. Where Keith lived, however, no one was known for anything except living, dying, or killing.

When some shocking event occurred, national attention was never brought to bear. Instead, the thing just happened. It ended, and then it happened again to someone else. Today was different. So although the reporter didn't know his name, and the artist's sketch looked nothing like him, Keith was in the papers. Keith Henry and his two friends had made headlines.

Keith leaned back in the driver's seat as smoke from the joint filled the idle car, slowly creeping its way from the back to the front. It captured the moonlight coming in through the surrounding bushes and illuminated the space inside the rust-red, four-door sedan with a gray haze. There was no traffic on the local highway, so the smoke was the only thing moving until Keith waved his hand at the joint that was passed to him. As always, he declined and continued to read the article.

The caption under the sketch read, "A manhunt is in effect for the murderers of Officer Jamison, Officer Daniels, and the two officers murdered last month." Exhaling deeply he folded the paper and threw it out of the driver's side window. With his huge frame buried in the passenger seat, Buck turned his head at Keith's heavy sigh. After taking a pull, he passed the joint to Shannon in the back and asked, "What up? Whatchu thinkin' 'bout?"

Keith seemed to ignore the question as he looked out the window with an unfocused gaze. He responded, "Thinking about what we've been doing."

"And?"

"I don't know. I don't feel sorry for what we did, or even that we should feel sorry. I'm just not sure if we should keep doing it." Raising his voice slightly, he continued, "I'm not talking about tonight. We're gonna get that piece of shit Douglas as soon as he hops out of his car. But some of these other guys though..." He trailed off and then said, "I mean, I never thought I'd be in a situation like this." He leaned his head back against the worn fabric of the headrest.

The car was the only thing his mother had left him after a second stroke put her in the grave. Keith rubbed his head against the stained nylon to remind himself of her. When she died, his mother was a fifty-seven-year-old nurse's aide, who had worked almost every day of her life since she was thirteen, but the only thing his mother left the world to prove she ever existed was him, the car they sat in, and his dead brother Blake. Indignation stirred in him, straightening his back and adding a determination to his voice. He said, "Forget it."

Buck said, "Nah, man. You got something to say, then say it."

"I'm fine."

"Aight yo. You still down to do this, right?"

"Yeah. Shannon, give me the list. Let's see who Douglas's partner is."

Shannon quietly passed a sheet of paper forward from the backseat. The paper was lined with thousands of soft wrinkles from having been balled up and flattened out repeatedly over the last two months.

Keith had asked Shannon, a legal aid clerk, to see if he could compile a list of Suffolk County police officers with the highest number of registered civilian complaints. Officer Douglas was number six from the top of the list. When Keith saw his name for the first time, he wrapped his long fingers around the paper as he said thank you to Shannon—giving the printout its first set of wrinkles.

###

The verdict was not guilty. Before the jury foreman said the last syllable, there were cries, shouts, and calls for order from the judge. Keith was in the middle of it, both emotionally and physically, as he sat at the third row and ground his teeth to keep from screaming threats or rushing the defendant's table.

Later that evening, Shannon and Keith talked about Officer Douglas's trial over a bottle of vodka and a carton of orange juice. Rain battered Keith's kitchen windows and created a white noise that filled the long silences. When they did speak, it was in slurred curse words that betrayed the poison they had been drinking by the glassful.

Keith stared at his reflection in the window. He and Blake looked so much alike and, as he had done since childhood, he noticed the similarity in their slim frames, their almond-shaped eyes, and even their unintentionally crooked smiles. They both looked like their mother, but now Keith was the only one left of the three. Each had been stolen from him. The anger kept him up, but as the hours went by there was more orange juice than vodka in their cups and the two began telling stories.

"She gave him her number, but as soon as she got in the taxi, right in front of the club mind you, he gave this all-over body shake and deleted her number from his phone then and there."

Keith clapped and laughed at the same time. "Blake couldn't stand women with bad breath."

Shannon continued, "I ain't gonna lie though. Her breath was stank! Smelled like she'd be chewing on dirty jock straps." They both laughed this time—letting their bodies move on impulse and in joy. When the laughter died, Keith noticed Shannon's lips straightened as he looked down at the ground.

"I think about him every minute." Keith said, "It's not that he's gone. It's that I know he's gone forever, you know? It's not like he went on a vacation, or even moved to another country. He's just gone. My brother doesn't exist anymore." Keith exhaled with a quiet roar that he felt rumbling in the back of his throat. His words quickened as he said, "It's like he just disappeared and all these pictures I have in my head of him learning to tie his shoelaces, getting in his first fight, smiling when he got his car… they're all I have to remind me that I had a brother." Shannon nodded, and Keith could see that he was holding back tears.

With the cup of mostly juice in his hand, Keith leaned back into the kitchen chair. "I can't believe what the hell happened yesterday. Five people saw that piece of shit shoot Blake in the back of the head, and he's not guilty." Shannon quietly shook his head in disbelief. "Not fucking guilty!" With his last word, Keith threw his cup on the kitchen floor. The porcelain shattered to pieces that flew in every direction—some heading towards Keith's face, though he didn't move, and his eyes didn't close.

Shannon ignored the mess on the floor. Finally, the tears streamed down his face, and he said, "I want them to feel what I feel."

Keith said, "I want them to feel what Blake felt."

###

Sitting in his mother's car with Buck and Shannon, Keith looked over the list of names and wondered about the dozens of complaints that put Officer Johnson—or any of the officers for that matter—on the list.

Did he shoot somebody? Did he beat up somebody? Was it a strip search? Maybe it was something as simple as a few illegal searches of Wyandanch residents who just looked guilty.

"How the fuck do you say this mothafuka's name?" Buck said. He leaned over to look at the list and, picked out Johnson's partner's name, "She warts. Sha warts. Wartz welder? This dude should get popped for that fucked up name alone." Keith smirked slightly, but Shannon's face remained as solemn as it had all night.

"That ain't funny." Shannon eventually said, "We're

gonna take the man's life. Nothing about this is a joke."

"C'mon man. It's a funny fucking name." Buck turned to Shannon in the back seat and smiled, but Shannon remained silent. "You for real?"

Buck turned around fully, placing his knees on his seat, and leaned over it to look Shannon in the eyes. The seat bent back and made a strained squeak, as if on the verge of snapping under Buck's massive frame. He said, "Yo, Schwarzenegger, or whateva the fuck his name is, is probably laughing right now after smashing some nigga's face on the sidewalk. You sitting here worrying about me disrespectin', and the dude is getting paid to beat on anyone he don't like. So why you care? Man, he ain't shit. That's why we gonna pop him tonight with that mothafuka Douglas."

Shannon said calmly, "If they laugh, that doesn't mean we have to. We're not them, and the reason we out here isn't the same reason they have for smashing someone's face into the concrete. I don't find anything funny about this."

"C'mon man. What do you think this is? Some kinda holy mission? Nigga, this ain't the crusades. We gonna kill 'em cuz they been killing us. One of 'em was trying to choke me to death." Banging hard on an armrest between him and Keith he said, "One of 'em put Blake in a fuckin' casket."

"Hey!" Keith shouted. "Calm the fuck down. We're doing this because it needs to be done. Just like last time. Now sit the hell back down before someone driving through remembers seeing a bunch of black guys fighting in a car."

Buck turned back around in his seat. In a low tone, he said, "Y'all niggas blowin' my high right now," and then took one last pull on the joint before putting it out. Keith kept an eye on Shannon through the rearview mirror, then he turned to Buck who began to touch the small, unnatural dimples on the skin of his neck. They were scars, and there were two, and each appeared just an open palm's length away from the other.

Keith was there the day Buck got them and thought about the sight of his friend being held to the ground by two cops while being choked by a third. Since then he would see Buck reflexively touch the marks every so often and grimace, almost without thinking. Starting last month, though, he would purposefully massage them to remind himself that the person who gave him the scars was no more. After rubbing them for a few seconds, Buck coughed and relaxed, leaving Keith to assume that the weed, along with the feelings of satisfaction from murder, calmed both Buck's body and mind.

Glossing over what the look of quenched bloodlust said about his own desires, Keith sat in the parked car, hidden behind a row of bushes along a barely traveled road, waiting quietly for the men on the list to come. He thought twice about the newspaper he had been handling all day. Opening the door slightly, he picked it up off the ground and threw it on the dashboard.

###

Earlier that morning while getting a haircut, Sam, Keith's barber, asked him, "You saw the Post today?"

Keith thought about how to answer the yes-or-no question. He didn't read the paper for the same reasons he rarely paid attention to television news. The newspapers were a place where celebrities took selfies, and where powerful white men made what were usually described as honorable, if not sometimes misguided, decisions. Keith

121

and his neighbors made decisions that impacted only them and the circle of people around them whose circumference reflected the amount of money they had or their connection to that world of the newspapers.

Keith wanted to say, "Fuck no," when asked about the Post, but he replied, "Nope. Why? You wanna know your horoscope?"

"Nah. The front page was about those cops who were killed."

"So? It was on TV too. Was there anything different in the papers?"

"No." Sam said. He paused and adjusted his glasses. "That's why I ask if you read it. If you had, you'd notice that nothing new was said. It was the same thing on the TV, the same thing online." Keith puckered his lips while waiting for some point to what was being said. "And it's sad cause they all keep repeating the same thing: what his family got to say and what the mayor got to say, but none of those reporters ever came around to ask us anything about that cop. I haven't seen one camera.

"That Officer Jamison patrolled this place for years. I seen him, more than once, holding down some young man to the floor with his knee in their back, telling whatever crowd gathers round that the boy has drugs. He got at your friend Buck a few times too, I think. Now, someone killed the man and all they can talk about is how his wife feels. You get what I'm saying to you?"

A younger barber looked up from the half-shaven scalp in front of him and said, "Yeah man, I hear you. I saw that mess on TV last night and, with all due respect, I don't care how his wife feel."

Noises of agreement came from others in the shop, but

most just nodded. Sam said, "Well, I wasn't saying that. The woman's been through something I don't wish on no one. What I'm trying to point out is that nobody asked us what we thought, and we seen the man day in and day out."

The other barber nodded in agreement and Sam continued to talk while sharpening the edges of Keith's hairline. "As far as I know, the man was no good. But they never asked me about him. They hold a press conference and have the wife crying for the cameras, asking for justice. Then the papers put out some pictures that look like The Jackson Five without Jermaine or Michael, telling us we should go hunt these brothers down and call the police when we see 'em."

The barbershop erupted in laughter, but Keith just chuckled.

"Where they get those pictures anyway?" Sam asked.

"Some sketch artist drew 'em looking at those blurry-ass videos from the cop car." The younger barber replied.

"My tax dollars at work."

"So you don't think these guys need to be brought in?" Keith asked.

"I'm not saying that." Replied Sam, "I'm just saying that there are two sides of a story. And from what I can see, our side ain't getting told."

###

Shannon nudged Keith from behind and said, "I think I hear something."

"Give it here."

Shannon passed the earpiece for the scanner they had tuned to the police radio frequency. Keith listened then said, "You're right. Let's go." Shannon handed out flares, and the three of them got out of the car and headed towards the road. They lined the flares on one side of the road. After lighting the flares, they ran to the bushes, and there they waited for the sounds of a patrol car.

###

After their night of orange juice and tears, Shannon and Keith weren't sure what to do about how they felt. It was rage, but the rage was different for each of them.

For Keith, it wasn't only that he had lost the boy he helped raise into a man, but that his life had been a list of losses, of things that went wrong because of who he was and where he lived. Why was it that his best friend sold drugs for a living? Why was it that his brother was the one dead? Why was it that the only thing his mother could pass down to him was her beat-up old car?

For Shannon, the rage was specific. He had seen Blake murdered. While both of them were handcuffed, sitting calmly on the sidewalk, Shannon had seen the bullet enter his best friend's head. He had seen the life escape from Blake's eyes and the piss fill Blake's pants. He and Blake had graduated from elementary school together. When he was depressed, Blake was the only one who could snap him out of it. That person was now gone.

Buck had similar feelings about Blake's death, but his weren't new. He had friends who were killed before, and he had friends who were killers. He had seen death up close. Unlike Shannon or Keith, Buck never had anyone around him worthy of the label "family," and so his closest relationships were always hard to maintain. Other than rage, he was numb to emotions and moved on instinct. It was Buck who was the first to hear the car approaching.

###

Buck said, "Yo, it's them."

Tonight they were looking for a release for their rage. Whatever judgment was placed on their actions didn't change the motivations. The why was all they knew, and the why was all they cared about.

Soon they all heard the police car. Through leaves, they saw flashing lights approach the flares. Buck had his shotgun out while Shannon and Keith pulled out their pistols. The police car stopped. Buck fired through the open window, peppering the driver's face and neck with a spray of shot pellets. Shannon burst out of the bushes, shooting into him to make sure he was dead. Keith followed but shot at the officer on the passenger side before he had a chance to retaliate.

Though hit, the passenger did shoot back. His bullets pierced the car's thick front windshield and scattered the three men around the car. Buck hid behind the police cruiser, near the trunk. Shannon and Keith ducked low as well, but kept moving—Keith from the rear and Shannon around the front—to approach the passenger side door. Shots whizzed over their heads.

As they neared, the policeman flung open his door and stepped out, firing in Shannon's direction. He let out two shots before Keith began shooting at his exposed leg from behind. The second shot hit, and he fell onto the asphalt. Shannon's next shot caused him to drop his gun. Both of them stood over the officer, and Keith kicked his weapon away. Without a word, they shot him, over and over again.

The policeman lay on the ground among slowly expanding pools of blood from the shots aimed solely at his gun arm and his legs. The red borders of blood crept across the asphalt as he cried and twitched in pain. Keith shouted, "You can take the camera out now!" Buck got up from behind the police car and walked to its dashboard as Shannon and Keith kept watch on the bleeding policeman for any sudden moves. Keith bent down to look at the man whose crying died down slightly as their eyes met. Keith thought he could see a spark of recognition in Officer Douglas's face. Maybe the officer recognized the man who was at his murder trial—wearing a suit and a look of barely concealed hate.

Keith saw that spark. He nodded to confirm he was that man, then he stood. Both Keith and Shannon aimed at the officer's head and fired until they had nothing left in their clips. Even after the "click click" of their useless pistols signaled that they had finished, Keith kept pulling the trigger. His hand strangling the gun handle as his arm began to shake; his face tightened and reddened.

Looking up and away from the dead man, Keith let out a scream—a wild wail that filled the empty air. Shannon and Buck listened as Keith emptied himself into the night. The sound glued their feet to the ground and made their hearts pump harder, because they knew exactly what was behind it. It was an anger that was in them too, and it had been filling their hearts for as long as they could remember being alive. They heard Keith and couldn't do anything but understand as he emptied himself. With nothing more to give, Keith lowered his head. He breathed in deeply to refill himself with the cold air and the smell of death that now surrounded him.

"We gotta go!" Buck yelled.

Shannon grabbed Keith's shoulder and said, "Come on."

They ran to the car and managed to close the doors as Buck sped off. After about fifteen seconds they passed a car heading towards the scene. The adrenaline from the ordeal was still filling their bodies. Shannon looked at Keith and asked, "You all right?"

With his brows furrowed in anger, he said, "Yeah. I'm fine. It's done."

Shannon shook his head, crying along with Keith, and said, "No. It's not done. We're not done."

Keith was silent. He looked at Buck, who looked back at him from the corner of his eye as he drove. Keith turned to Shannon and said, "You're right. It's not done." As Buck continued speeding back to Wyandanch, Keith repeated, for himself and for the others, "No, it's not over."

SUNSHINE

JOAN WOKE UP, but she was still asleep.

She snoozed the alarm on her smart phone and lay in bed a few minutes longer than she should have. The scent of fabric softener from the newly cleaned sheets filled her nose; though in her sleepy state Joan imagined she could also smell the metallic tinge of blood from the time she split her lip learning how to ride a bicycle. It took more than a few encouraging words to get her back on, but she eventually learned to ride a big girl's bike. That was forty-five years ago, but in her mind the scene was as fresh as the bed sheets over her face; the memory was as real as the grating knowledge that she needed to get out of bed.

In time, Joan rolled herself out of bed and walked through her almost pitch-black apartment with both eyes closed. She clumsily moved toward the bathroom along with dreams that clung to her body like smoke. Joan peed and wondered if her husband was still alive in some way, like a television show angel or a ghost. He hovered above to keep her safe from collapsing buildings and low flying airplanes. Maybe when she was at her lowest point—deliriously crying in bed and grasping at his side of it—Aidan whispered in her ear that he was still there.

For a moment, she thought she could hear him in the shower, washing off the day's dirt and laughing at some random thought that he would tell her about while scrubbing his leg. After a decade and a half, she still remembered the sound of his laugh. His laughs were more like good-natured chuckles and came with a confident smile that made him seem invincible. He was invincible, and then he died.

Joan wiped herself and, after flushing, blindly groped for her toothbrush. After the practiced routine of jabbing its paste-covered head into her mouth, she slipped into a daydream where she had won the lottery. She ran home with two garbage bags filled with money, and a mouth tasting like mint. Joan told Aidan they were quitting their jobs and going on a trip around the world. He lifted her off the ground with ease and told her he was going to go to work that day because there would be chaos in the city and he had to get people out of harm's way—away from the fallen towers. Aidan smiled and said that he would always love her.

Joan spit into the sink and almost fell in as she leaned the weight of her upper body on the porcelain edge to rinse her mouth. She was tired from the night of hosting. Several friends and family members listened to music, drank, and told stories. Charles talked about the recent police versus firefighter charity boxing event and said that if "Aidan were there, he'd have busted the faces of at least eight or ten cops. No help at all." Everybody agreed with loud cheers and held their bottle or glass in the air.

Right before the last drink was poured and guests petered out, Charles caught Joan in the kitchen as she was bringing a bottle of whiskey into the living room. He said, "You asked why me and Emily were late. Well, I wasn't sure I was going to come today."

"Why wouldn't you?"

"I'm just not sure this is, you know, that this is healthy for you. We all want to remember Aiden," Charles puckered his lips and furrowed his brow before continuing, "but maybe it's not the best thing for our little get-togethers to be at your place. I feel like we reopen old wounds."

"Don't be silly, Charlie. This was Aiden's place as much as mine and his friends are always welcome." She put the whiskey bottle on the kitchen counter. "Besides what makes you think I don't want to remember Aiden too? I... you know what he meant to me. And hearing you guys talk about him is one of the only things that keeps him alive. If it's just me, Charlie, I might forget those little bits and pieces that made him special. It helps remembering him through you guys. Aiden was so much bigger than what I remember and I just need to have that confirmed." A few tears began to fall and she leaned on the counter for support. Her voice trembled slightly as she said, "I need to hear that Aiden was more than the fading memories I have of him."

Charles glanced at the floor and then, looking back at Joan, said, "I understand." From the kitchen they walked into the midst of an Aiden story that broke into cheers when Joan showed off the new bottle and smiled. Of course, the parties had grown smaller over the years, but it was still large, Aidan being so well loved.

The annual September gatherings were something Joan both enjoyed and hated. She wanted to remember her husband the way the others did in their stories. Aidan was strong and self-assured. He was brave. Joan remembered that Aidan was also incredibly gentle. He would kiss the back of her neck when she wasn't expecting it. He often fell asleep with his head on her chest with his straight black hair twisted around her fingers. Aiden radiated a contagious compassion and warmth that she had never seen before or since.

She missed him in ways she couldn't share. She missed the way he made love to her. The way he held her and looked into her eyes made Joan feel like the most precious person on the planet. She kept these stories to herself, just as she cried to herself when the last guest left.

After she closed the door behind them, Joan had pulled the thick window shades together and she kept them closed after she got out of bed. They maintained a darkness in the St. George condo that made it easy for her to dream as she walked out of the bathroom. With each step to the window, she imagined new lives and different places where happiness could be found. Wild adventures that would distract her forever from her loss. Eventually, however, she opened her eyes and pulled back the shades to let the sun shine in.

She could see the lower Manhattan skyline from her window, bathed in morning light. The sight was beautiful, and although its brightness stung her eyes, she looked ahead until she was used to it. In the dark Joan remained separated from reality, but in the sun she was forced to realize that the world was bigger than her, her grief, or her city.

The day had begun. To make up for lost time Joan quickly got dressed and left to meet her boyfriend for breakfast.

DEAD LABOR

I LEANED AGAINST A DISPLAY of computer towers and computer-printed price tags on my fifth day in a row at that place that I didn't want to be. A bank was holding me hostage downtown between Trinity and Broadway. If I left they would starve me. They would let sickness consume me. They would have me freeze under a bridge—food for vultures with bad habits.

I had begun to see things a little differently after having five years of five days in a row. Close objects had become distant as my mind went in and out of focus for hours at a time while being paid by the hour to do something I didn't want to do. I was able to tell the time by looking at shadows cast by the natural light that somehow found its way inside that building of concrete and dead labor —the cash register became a sundial. At four o'clock I began to realize how soft my mind had become, really, how malleable

ALEX CLERMONT

reality itself was, and I began wondering about the world around me.

I could feel a customer approaching as I stared at the register to check, one more time, when and where I was.

I thought, if I punch a glass window. If I punched a decently thick glass window with enough force, but also with enough speed, I think I could kinda catch it off guard and bend it, like metal or something.

I said, "How can I help you, sir?"

I thought, if someone has a face like an animal, what does that mean? Maybe the animal that they look like is their totem—their animal guide in this world. This man has the spirit of the platypus looking after him, I think. It makes sure he will never drown. It means he's unique, like a platypus, and that others will view his existence with skepticism until they can hold him and touch his smooth face. Maybe his platypus spirit is watching me, looking into my soul and forcing me to tell him things I don't want to. I hate platypuses. Jigsaw animals.

I said, "Well, it's not on the shelves, but sometimes items we've just received don't get put out on the sales floor till much later. I'll see if we have that in stock somewhere in the back. Give me a few while I check?"

I heard the customer say, "Sure."

I thought, if I could run fast enough, with my arms spread and tilted at just the right angle, I might be able to get some lift.

I heard the inventory manager say, "Nah, we don't got that in stock. Best bet for him would be to order it to this store and pick it up, or have it delivered to his place."

I said, "All right. I'll let him know."

I thought, I'm about ninety percent water. If I had to

guess I'd say the rest of me is made up of stuff like iron, potassium… probably some bullshit like aluminum. All told, they're pretty cheap. I wonder how much I would be worth if I was on the shelf next to the laptops? Fifteen dollars? Ten?

I said, "Okay, sir, would you like to pick it up or have it delivered to your home? Just so you know, you would get free delivery to your home since you're using your store credit card."

I heard the customer say, "Really? That sounds great. Can I get it delivered to my house then?"

I said, "Sure. Give me a second while I pull up your information."

I thought, everything I see is just reflected light, but even light has a speed limit, right? It's fast, but it has a limit. It takes time for that light to reach my eyes even though I think it's instant. So, if the light I see bouncing off something is old, even by a nanosecond, then everything I'm seeing happened in the past. Nothing I see is happening at this moment—right now. Right now only happens when I touch something. When I'm in direct contact. That's where it's at. Direct contact, not seeing, is what's real.

I said, "Have a good day sir."

I heard the customer say, "You too. Thanks a lot for your help."

I said, "No problem."

I thought, I can't stay here anymore. This job is gonna drive me insane.

I thought, I have to find something new.

As the customer walked away I slowly took off the uniformed shirt that someone else had sewn in a factory a continent away while being held hostage, as I was. I folded it neatly into the drawer under the LCD screens. Deciding to leave that place I didn't want to be in, I walked through the revolving door and into the outside world. I wouldn't be a hostage anymore, but I wouldn't die either. I'd find something new, something real.

HUNGRY GHOSTS OF PARK AVENUE

THE VIEW FROM the Park Avenue penthouse apartment was gorgeous. Carl noticed it immediately that first night at Phil's when he stepped out of the private elevator and into the partly crowded cocktail party. The front tips of Carl's shoes touched the base of the floor-to-ceiling window as he stood there, mesmerized by the vastness of New York City's streets. The towering, wide-angle view of the world was almost spiritual in that it impressed upon him the gut feeling that things seen and unseen were all connected.

There was no Lexington or Thirty-fourth. Names didn't matter as asphalt roads morphed into dissected veins, glowing red or blue-white with light from the cars that flowed through them like blood. He could even see over the Hudson River into New Jersey. Borders between places broke down and Carl saw it all as one. The streets were all one, the land was all one, the people—with their almost identical features of heads, arms and legs—were all one. Carl smiled for the first time in a long time until Reggie tapped him on the shoulder and said, "Yo. This motherfucka's giving out coke like it's candy. You better get some."

Carl turned his head away from the one to look at the many people who filled the apartment. He didn't feel completely comfortable walking around them. They looked cold and almost aristocratic in their bearing—the type of people who may murder as a by-product of a power grab. Carl and Reggie were dressed in clean but shabby clothes that had been worn and washed and worn many times before. Compared to the crisp blazers and pretty dresses around them, Carl felt out of place.

He said so earlier, but Reggie dismissed it with, "Nigga, please. We gonna have a good time." Despite the fact that he was white, Carl went along with the label and the plan of action.

This short verbal exchange was a real world recreation of the relationship they forged while in the man-made world of prison. Inside, Reggie talked with a lisp and got the attention of men who hadn't seen a woman in years. Carl wasn't one of those men, but the two became friends behind bars and met up again after being released. After hanging out together in shelters and rehab clinics for six months, Reggie began a relationship with a high-class addict who later invited them to his Midtown home for drinks.

After being tapped on his shoulder that first night at that apartment, Carl asked Reggie, "Are you fucking this guy?"

"What you think?"

"I don't want to assume."

As they walked toward the center of what Carl would

call the fourth living room, Reggie said over his shoulder, "Yeah, we fucking. It ain't nothing. He likes taking care of me. Makes him feel good. Let's just get what we can out of it while it lasts."

Carl looked around at the high ceilings, Victorian-style furniture, and pretty chandeliers. He shrugged his shoulders in agreement. He didn't like the idea of Reggie whoring himself out, but that was the nature of freedom, such as they had it. Reggie had choices and he was free to choose whoring.

Phil greeted them with a smile and open arms. His Gieves & Hawkes cashmere blazer and crewneck sweater were both midnight black and gave the impression that his upper body was a dark void with disconnected hands and a head on top. His smile was possessed with a slight mania and when he reached Reggie, he kissed him full on the lips in front of the mingling guests—many of whom raised their eyebrows or giggled to themselves. Phil's chemically fueled tunnel vision led his focus from Reggie to Carl, who he met with a bear hug full of familiarity. His smile remained as he asked, "So you guys want some coke?"

Reggie laughed as he said, "Fuck yeah."

The three walked a short distance to a table. On it was a small pile of cocaine that Carl guessed to be about half a pound. Next to it were some playing cards, one of which Reggie grabbed and used to separate himself a thick line as Phil asked Carl, "How do you like the place?"

"It's extremely nice. I was just admiring the view. You must stand there for hours whenever you have a day off or something."

"I don't have..." The sound of Reggie's snorting filled Carl's ears. "... days off. Don't look out the window much either, I'm afraid. I guess I'm just too used to it."

Reggie lifted his head from above the table and interrupted, "The man is rich, Carl. I told you that."

"That doesn't mean he can't take a day off once in a while," Carl responded, a little annoyed at the tone of Reggie's interjection.

"No, Reggie's right. I don't *have* a job to take days off from, and that's *because* I'm rich. You can call me a trust fund baby if you'd like."

Between lines Phil gave Carl a quick biography that included being lucky enough to be born to a mother who was born to a grandfather who helped found the public relations industry in America. His claim to fame was cleaning up the reputation of a national mining company after its owner hired local police to shoot into a crowd of striking workers and their families. He published industry articles and books that called the general population stupid sheep. He made millions.

Phil was raised without a care and that was part of the story he told Carl. Reggie laughed loudly, and often, at whatever part of the life story was said with wit. Phil was charming and handsome, with loose curls of salt and pepper hair. Carl wondered why he was seeing Reggie who, in his straight eyes, was also handsome but had the same air of working-class poverty that Carl had.

Again, not wanting to assume, he left the mystery where it was and bent over to do a line. The immediate rush made him jolt his head back and rub his nose. Phil and Reggie had disappeared into the small crowd of guests who fluttered about the spacious main room with its high ceilings and transformative views.

Beginning to feel the drip at the back of his throat, Carl

looked around with excited eyes. He noticed some of the strange looks he was receiving, but began to look right back as he stared at breasts and asses. It was a temporary spike in libido that was an exception rather than the rule in his life since prison.

He had been a mechanic who thought that stealing high-end cars in Long Island made more sense than fixing low-end ones in Queens. For five years he was right, and he had sent many a luxury vehicle to overseas clients in shipment containers. A Porsche 911 Carrera became his downfall, and he spent five years with people like Reggie, whose own crime was being unlucky enough to be born to poor parents and taking drugs to forget that fact.

Phil's quality cocaine raised Carl's dopamine levels along with his erection. *I'm not that ugly either*, he thought as he kept staring at body parts. His eyes eventually landed on a woman who struck the perfect balance of attainable but attractive. Feeling fantastically confident he walked up to her and said, "This is my first time in Phil's apartment, but I'm hoping he'll give it to me if I'm nice enough to him."

She smiled politely and said, "If only it were that easy."

"I'm persistent. And my name's Carl." Carl reached his hand out to the woman.

She grabbed it and said, "Nancy."

"Hi, Nancy. So, how do you know Phil?"

"I only know him by association. My friend is his wealth manager."

"You mean, like an accountant."

Nancy looked downward with a patronizing smile that Carl noticed but didn't care about. "Something like that," she said. "I saw you and your friend earlier. You guys sure do make an entrance."

"Him more than me. I'm the quiet one."

"So how do *you* know Phil?"

"Same as you. Through my friend."

"And how does your friend know him?"

"He and Phil regularly have sex. At least that's how I understand it." Carl grabbed a champagne flute off a passing waiter's tray. Nancy pursed her lips slightly in embarrassment.

She said, "Well, that's pretty blunt."

"I wouldn't think Phil would fault me for it. Someone who has two handfuls of cocaine on his living room table in the middle of a party isn't one for social graces. Or at least not ones we're used to."

Nancy laughed as Carl bent his head back a little and nonchalantly drank half the glass. The bubbles burned his throat, but they tasted good so he didn't mind. He heard Nancy say, "You're absolutely right, Carl." His dick moved at the sound of his name. "Phil is a little eccentric."

"That's one way to describe it. I think it's admirable though."

"Why so?"

"Well, in his case at least, it's made him pretty down to earth. That is to say, he's not pretentious. To have as much money as he obviously does and not look down on my friend is kind of rare. I would imagine it's rare anyway." He looked Nancy in the eyes as he talked.

She said, "Maybe you're right."

"Hopefully. Who likes to be wrong? Hey, did you try the…" Carl pointed his thumb at the flat tabletop.

"No. I haven't."

"Do you not…" Carl trailed off again, implying words that may have assumed too much if said out loud.

"Yeah, a few times. I like it, but you can get lost in that stuff if you're not careful."

"I think any vice, in moderation, is perfectly fine. C'mon. Let's do a line off Phil's genuine marble table. We may never get the opportunity again." Nancy giggled as she followed him to the end of the room, grabbing her own champagne flute from another passing server.

They each did two lines, but with a lot of talk between each snort. Nancy's expressions loosened as Carl spoke about observations that made her giggle. It was the coke talking. In general Carl didn't bother with the opposite sex other than what was required of him in places like clinics and benefits centers. He remembered liking sex before prison, but his desire to pursue most things, whether a career or pussy, had deflated against the stronger desire to do nothing.

In Riker's island jail, and then later in prison, Carl was a nobody. He liked it that way. He never got involved in any disputes over sleeping arrangements or commissary items or lunch privileges. He used his mouth for breathing, not talking. What he couldn't avoid, however, was the madness around him. He had seen an inmate overdose on drugs sold to him by prison doctors. He had seen somebody's cheek gashed open with the thin edge of a lunch tray. Carl had seen the blood-soaked pants of a prisoner who claimed that guards had gang raped him just minutes before. That prisoner was Reggie and, while Carl tried to keep a low profile, the two shared a starved need for human kindness that made them friends and fellow addicts for want of an escape plan from life's horrors.

Carl was sure Nancy had a much tamer version of the same story. If not, then why the two lines? Why the increasingly sexual flirting?

Carl knew from experience that despite their negative effects, quitting drugs was only something done in the context of alternatives. You needed something better. To feel the love and happiness lacking in his real life Carl sniffed cocaine, he shot up heroine, he smoked meth—though only occasionally.

He didn't want to get in Nancy's head too much so he said, "Phil neglected to offer me a tour of the place. I volunteer you for it."

"Is that so? I've never been volunteered for anything before."

"It'll be fun. I promise."

Carl rarely smiled. Mainly because his teeth weren't in great shape, but with Nancy he also avoided it to add an air of aloofness that he could tell she wanted. He only smirked and did so as he waved her away from the crowd and toward one of the hallways. He had no knowledge of the apartment's layout but figured that if they wandered around enough an area without people would show itself.

As they slowly drifted from one area of the apartment to the next, Carl made conversation and asked Nancy what she did for a living. She said she worked for a major electronics company as the head of its in-house graphic design team. She helped design product packaging, among other things. Carl was sincerely interested as he looked for the next available turn. He asked if she enjoyed it. She said she enjoyed it immensely. She admitted, though, that her personal life suffered for it. Her office was her primary home, turning her real home into nothing but an expensive box with a bed on the Upper East Side.

Carl said, "We all chase something. The best you can do

is at least be aware of what it is you're going to catch." Carl thought that sounded profound. The two stepped into a large broom closet where they began making out.

Though his teeth were not in great shape, Carl's breath smelled like mint. He religiously showered and always wore cologne. They were all attempts at covering up the fact that he moved from place to place and occasionally lived in a men's shelter or a cheap Bronx motel. Carl and Reggie traveled around New York City like a scripted buddy drama as they stole, injected, laughed, and continued to draw breath despite themselves.

While fucking Nancy on the closet floor, he began to disassociate. Stepping outside of the moment, Carl saw himself and asked what, exactly, was making sex with Nancy feel so good. For one he enjoyed the feeling of her warmth against his body—the heat was recognition that another human was touching him. Also Nancy's tightness as she held him inside felt glorious. Maybe most importantly, however, there were the moans of pleasure that let him know he was good. Carl liked being reassured that he was good at something.

The whole experience was wonderful, and like the cocaine high, he wished it would last forever. That was always impossible and he felt the end coming as Nancy wrapped her arms around his neck and lifted herself off the ground from her former missionary position. She began to silently tear over what Carl recognized as some hidden trauma. He sat up, grabbed her tight, and slowly grinded her hips against his as he said, "I've got you. You're safe." She grabbed him even tighter and he could feel her come. After a few quivers, she relaxed and kissed him slowly on the lips.

"Damn, you're good," she said in one breath. He soaked

in the compliment. He felt it on his skin like a cooling balm and smiled slightly as Nancy stood up. She picked up one of her fallen diamond earrings from the floor and sniffed up a few last tears as Carl removed the condom she had given him to wear.

"C'mon." she said. "Let's head out. The tour isn't over."

They walked through the remaining rooms and halls of the penthouse. They had sex again in one of the studies then walked back to the crowded main rooms where they continued talking. They had more champagne.

After some time had passed, they were greeted by Phil who also had his fingers wrapped around the stem of a champagne flute. He had as much energy as before but looked slightly disheveled. The black void of his blazer and sweater was disturbed by the white of an undershirt poking out from beneath his collar.

As if they had just met, Phil gave Carl a huge hug and kissed Nancy on the left cheek. Carl asked, "Where's Reggie?"

"Oh he's passed out in the bedroom. How are *you* two? Enjoying everything? You know, I was going to get a DJ, but I thought that would really kill the vibe in here. I want people to hear *people*, not some pre-recorded, electronic blips and bumps. Do you think I made a bad decision?"

Nancy said, "I think everyone's having a great time."

"That's what I want to hear!" His eyes darted around for a moment and he said, "Nancy, I think I see your friend James. Let me see if I can grab his ear for a second." Looking back at them he said, "But before I do, let's have a toast." Phil raised his half-full glass to meet with Carl's and Nancy's. "May we get all we want and more!"

As soon as the glasses clinked Phil moved on. Carl thought

it was a fine toast and drank slowly as he and Nancy walked to the window to cast their eyes on the city.

That first night at Phil's home was almost perfect. The nights continued, however, and eventually turned to weeks. Weeks turned to months, and one morning Carl woke up on a couch in his underwear with dried blood from his nose covering his mouth and jaw in a scabby crust. Time had flown by, but as he slowly sat up all Carl could think of was that first night.

Whatever he and Nancy shared was short lived. They exchanged phone numbers but neither called the other. Reggie and Phil started seriously getting into heroin. Carl began increasing his dosage as well but not to the level of those two, who needed to shoot up in the morning just to get out of bed.

Still groggy from the night before, Carl got up and walked around in what could have looked like purposeless steps as the vague feeling of hunger slowly drove him to the kitchen. He could hear echoes of rough sex from the master bedroom. It was Phil, Reggie, and maybe another guest. There were moans of pain and Carl involuntarily remembered a scene from two weeks ago where he walked into the room and saw Reggie penetrating Phil from behind while a skinny, milk-skinned woman grabbed his curly hair and thrust her baby-sized right fist into his throat.

Carl wasn't sure what he was looking for. He aimlessly dug through the refrigerator until his palm hit a carton of lemonade. Grabbing it, he walked back to the same couch he had just slid off. He put his mouth on the carton opening, but stopped short of drinking when he suddenly noticed the ridge feeling of his skin. He turned left to see his reflection in the hallway mirror, which showed him the crimson mask that covered his lower face. He was disgusted but not shocked at the sight of what was around his mouth. He sighed and as his shoulders dropped so did his head.

What had been driving Carl was instinct. He felt, from the fog of his subconscious, problems that he was constantly trying to fix but just couldn't because he didn't have the right tools. If Reggie took time out from shooting up and asked him what would make him happy, Carl probably wouldn't have an answer. Not a real answer anyway. Not one that would satiate his needs and leave him feeling content for more than a few hours. Indeed looking at his wilted figure and scabbed face Carl realized that the happiness he had gained at Phil's had worn thin long ago. Carl had no other solutions forthcoming to soothe the unnamed pains that drove his actions.

When he was stealing cars he loved the thrill of doing something illegal. He craved the attention that flashing money got him. Most important, though, was the knowledge that his life was wholly his and that the decisions he made were not directed from on high. After that power was taken from him, drugs provided an easy escape from the cage he was in. The end result wasn't hard to predict and Carl could see it quite clearly in his own reflection.

He felt hurt and walked a little slower to the massive window he had noticed that first night. The beauty he had seen then was gone. Past the thick glass, there was just concrete, dirt, and dirty people who moved like they were possessed by unseen forces that dragged their legs left and right.

DARK PLACES

It was robbing season where I worked. Although I didn't know why, it seemed a demonstrable fact that the warmth of summer somehow thawed the laziness of low-level criminals. Cops patrolled more often, random beatings became more frequent, and stick-up men looked for anything that shined with a focus that would be inspiring if it was directed at a book.

I don't think Doug knew or thought about any of that though. In his typically unenergetic voice, our manager asked us to work after closing time on a Friday night. The temptation of overtime pay was too much for our hungry wallets to resist and so most of us stayed late, despite the dangers outside.

Two other money-starved employees and I were told to clear the sales floor of all merchandise. It was going to be waxed or buffed, or both, and from what I gathered the flooring company offered a discount if they didn't have to move anything. The amount they discounted was more than what would be needed to pay *us* to move stuff. The arithmetic probably took Doug all of three seconds so in accordance with his sound math we pushed carts of sleeping pills and dumped boxes of energy drinks into the gated lot behind the store. We all did the work on the cheap for the company—though every one of us thought we were getting over.

Overtime pay made Jackie stay, though barely. She told me she was a little scared of the neighborhood. She said that she wasn't sure if the gates were high enough to keep out the wildness that the prospect of free pharmaceuticals might bring. We wouldn't leave until two in the morning and she whispered embarrassingly that she never liked being around past 10 p.m. I grew up in the neighborhood though. I knew it like a close relative. And I knew that, at night, the gates would *definitely* not be high enough to keep out thieves for more than a few hours. Luckily a few hours was all the time we needed.

We emptied the store of all its unshelved items in under an hour while Doug sat in the manager's office to organize paperwork and check his social media feeds. With a box of unpacked cough syrup in my arms, I snuck a peek of him looking through a Facebook page called "Big Ol' Booties." He scrolled down its timeline, which was filled with a mix of candid and professional photos of women's asses. Even with my passing glance, I could see Photoshop at work. Someone was using smudge tools, alpha layers, lightening and darkening effects to carve out perfect butts that could never exist in the real world. Though I didn't like it, I admired the fact that he was able to surf the net for borderline porn while I worked.

After setting the last of the products outside, we waited. In folding chairs we removed from the break room, Jackie, Daryl, and I sat around in anticipation. The waxer would soon be there, and afterwards we would undo the last forty-five minutes of work by putting boxes of product back inside the store. While sitting in the small lot, we chit-chatted.

I hated the small talk, but Jackie seemed uncomfortable being quiet so she asked questions and made comments that I felt inclined to respond to. Daryl leaned back in his chair and pretended to sleep. Though his eyes were closed, I could hear Dance Hall Reggae leaking out of his headphones, and I could see his hands moving rhythmically in his baggy pants pockets as he drummed the beat on his thigh. I had no excuse so I answered Jackie when she asked why I worked there.

My answer was short, but true. I lived a few blocks away and they were hiring. The hours worked with my hectic college sophomore schedule, but that was just a nice bonus. I told her there was no specific reason for me deciding to work there, at least no more than any other place that paid in US dollars. She didn't seem to understand. Her suddenly bluer eyes squinted a bit, and she told me that she started working there a few weeks ago because she had a dual major of pharmacology and business. She couldn't get an internship as a freshman, but since Doug was a second cousin and could get her the job she figured this would be a good substitute. She said some more things, but I didn't pay much attention to them.

Jackie didn't notice and kept our conversation alive with naïve questions about East Flatbush and what it was like growing up around here. She lived with her nuclear family in Park Slope, where they owned a brownstone that had probably quadrupled in value since they moved in. Her walks to the grocery on Fifth Avenue for organic, non-GMO, gluten-free, vegan, tofu eggs was nothing like walking on Farragut Road.

The differences between the two places weren't hard to spot, and once robbing season had begun, even Jackie saw it. She wanted me to tell her my thoughts on why things were so unsafe. Why did the people act the way they did? I answered her questions with short sentences that said nothing important. I didn't feel like being her black friend that day. My empty remarks were peppered with yawns as minutes flew by and I started missing my bed. Soon, though, the van from the flooring service arrived.

Doug came out just as I unlocked the gate, letting the van drive in. The one-man crew hopped out of the driver's side as soon as the car was in park. His light-brown hair was a tossed mess and his reddish beard was equally unkempt. His eyes shifted slightly from left to right and his uniform was stained in odd places. Judging a book by its cover, I guessed that he probably stunk too. Doug was the one walking him inside so I made a mental note to ask him about the waxer's smell. These were the stupid things that filled my mind at midnight.

I sat back down and decided to have some fun with Jackie. I told her about a time I was robbed.

I began with the fact that I was in high school at the time and coming home late after stopping by a friend's house to help him improve his shitty math skills. How shitty? Real shitty. Shitty to the point where you wondered how he functioned in the real world without some kind of specially trained math dog to bark at him when it was time to carry the one. Had the streetlights been working, they would've turned on a few minutes before I decided to take a shortcut home through a church parking lot.

Guessing what was next Jackie gasped at the unimaginable idea of a crime happening on church grounds. I asked her to stick to nail biting and hold any comments until the end of the story.

A fact that I hadn't mentioned to her was that it was the church I was baptized in. It was the one my parents praised Jesus in and where they got on their knees on Sundays to beg God for money while putting five dollars in the collection basket. I walked through its parking lot when I passed by three guys who were talking and laughing near a parked car. I didn't pay them much attention until I noticed, from the corner of my eye, one of them walking towards me from behind. Jackie's body stiffened when I said that I understood immediately what was going on and ran. Of course they caught up to me.

One of them punched me in the back of the head and I fell onto the concrete sidewalk. The second I was down I felt kicks and punches that I instinctively tried to avoid by curling up in the fetal position—my forehead touching my knees between my bent arms. I felt my book bag being pulled away and my pockets being dug into as they shouted angry words at me. When they were done they walked away, leaving me bloody in front of the church steps. When I was sure that the group was gone, I got up and walked home.

Jackie seemed shaken up by the story. In reaction I chuckled and told her that I lived in a dangerous area. She stopped talking and I took the opportunity to relax while the floor was being buffed or waxed.

We were about ten feet away from a gate that faced the sidewalk. Through its holes I could see people coming and going. The numbers of passersby were less than they were a few hours before, but the subway exit down the street still let out the occasional group of mainly black folks. Jackie was scared of them. She didn't know she was scared of them and if confronted she would probably deny it, but she was. By seeming coincidence they lived in the city's dark places. And with only coincidence she was forced to draw her own conclusions about why that was the case.

She was a little scared of me too, probably. It was the questions she asked and the tone of her voice that let me know. With a sort of surprised patronization—as if I used the wrong dinner fork—Jackie told me that the people in East Flatbush didn't live as well as the people of Brooklyn Heights or Downtown Manhattan because of some unspoken flaw. If I passed her on any given street or sidewalk, and she didn't recognize me, her muscles would tense up and her mind would fill itself with the millions of police sketches she'd seen of scary men with dark skin and thick lips.

It was nothing though. I dozed off.

After sleeping for I don't know how long, I woke up to the sounds of Doug and the floor guy arguing. I turned around and saw Doug standing near the back exit with his head cocked to the side, looking annoyed. The floor guy was flailing his arms and yelling at Doug about how he didn't care what discount he was told, he would have to pay the bill. Dismissively, Doug said that it wasn't *his* fault that the floor guy's manager, or whoever, didn't tell him what was going on. And it wasn't *his* fault that the shady company paid commissions and not a salary. He said that in the end though *he* didn't care and he wasn't going to pay anything higher than the number he was quoted earlier.

The floor guy let out a sound like a growl mixed with a scream. He grabbed something from his belt and then stuck it in Doug's chest, right below his left collarbone. The next second lasted a month, and I could see the crazed look on the floor guy's face, which was covered in sweat and twitching with a chemical rage I'd only seen once before—I was on the ground getting stomped on at the time. Jackie was screaming with shocked, wide-open eyes. Daryl was tucking in his chest while his shoulders heaved forward—as if catching an invisible football thrown low. It was a movement of pain sympathy that went along with a moan of *oh shit*. Doug was silent. He only looked down in disbelief at the thing that was poking out of his chest.

The second after that second went by pretty quickly. After finishing his *oh shit*, Daryl jumped out of his seat and rushed at the floor guy who was focused on the bleeding wound he had made in Doug's body. With the strength of his whole upper body, Daryl threw a quick punch that landed on the floor guy's face. He fell backwards, knocked his head onto the asphalt, and didn't get up. Doug also began to fall, though a little slower. First he fell to his knees, then he collapsed on his right side.

I ran to Doug to see if he was still breathing. He was. I pulled out my cell phone, dialed 911, and frantically looked Doug up and down while waiting for a response. What was sticking out of him was a slightly curved blade with a light brown wooden handle that Doug looked down at as he tried to talk. He couldn't and just kept slowly mouthing wet noises. Behind me I could hear Daryl call the floor guy a motherfucking dust head. I could also hear a crowd that had gathered by our gate, presumably from the train station and almost certainly attracted by Jackie's horror movie scream.

Jackie was yelling at me to take the knife out of Doug. I was about to when I heard someone from the crowd shouting at me not to. I looked for who that was, and as I told the 911 operator where we were I saw the man right outside the gate. He shouted that if I removed the blade I'd cause more bleeding. My brain overloaded and I just fell on my ass without a word. The operator told me to wait, and I did.

The man outside the gate climbed it until he was inside. He ran past Jackie to Doug, and while looking at Doug much less frantically than I did, he told me he was an EMS worker. I just nodded in agreement. He breathed into Doug's mouth and listened to the gurgling sounds that came up. He asked if anyone had a ballpoint pen or something. I handed him my Bic, which he snapped the ends off of. He pulled out his own pocketknife and sliced into Doug's chest a few inches below the blade. He stuck the hollowed pen in the new hole and listened again to Doug's breathing. He asked Doug if he was all right and Doug just looked at him for a moment or two. In a low whisper, he told him no, not really, and then smiled a little.

The EMS worker told me that since the wound was above Doug's heart I should keep him propped up a little so the gash wouldn't let out so much blood. As I lifted Doug's back off the ground, I could see Jackie walk toward us still scared out of her mind, but a level below screaming banshee.

We both looked at Doug who kept a slight smile on his face. Daryl was massaging his fist as he said that all of this was some crazy shit. Using different words Jackie said the same thing to the EMS worker who was slowly getting off his knees and back to his feet. He nodded in agreement and said that no matter where you live crazy shit could happen. There were a lot of dark places in New York City.

At that, Jackie and I looked at each other. She suddenly, and significantly, calmed down as the fear that was usually in her eyes disappeared. I also caught eye contact with Daryl, shaking his head, and Doug, wearing a placid smile. With a sweeping look I noticed the rest of the surroundings that I had taken for granted.

An ambulance was racing down the street, and as I looked at the EMS worker, I said, "They're everywhere, but we can all try our best to light them up."

Alex Clermont is a creative writer born and raised in New York City. He is the author of "You, Me and the Rest of Us: #NewYorkStories," "Eating Kimchi and Nodding Politely," along with dozens of several short stories and flash fiction. His stories have appeared in several literary journals and anthologies including *The Bodega Monthly*, *Black Elephant*, *The aois21 Annual*, *Every Second Sunday*, *Foliate Oak*, and *Out of Place*.

Website: AlexClermontWrites.com
Twitter: @AlexClermont
Facebook: Facebook.com/AlexClermontWrites
instagram: @AlexClermont